WHERE I
GRASS GOING?

To Dawne
Thankyou
Deborah . xx

D E Fox

First published in 2024 by Blossom Spring Publishing
Where Is All The Grass Going? Copyright © 2023 D E Fox
ISBN 978-1-0687019-7-9
E: admin@blossomspringpublishing.com
W: www.blossomspringpublishing.com

For Jake and Sammy, thank you for letting us
have you in our lives.
We are definitely better for it.

And a massive thank you to Clare.

"If there are no dogs in heaven, then when I die I want to go where they went."
Mark Twain.

1

"And they're off!" shouted the commentator as the horses bolted from the start. There were 40 horses battling to be the winner of *The Grand National*. The spectators, all with their posh suits and beautiful hats, looked on as the horses jumped over the first hurdle.

"Arghhhhhhh!" the commentators shouted as two horses fell, throwing their jockeys to the ground, each rolling into the smallest ball they could. The remaining horses kept going up the racecourse, bumping into each other as they steered around the bend. Gasps of horror came from the crowd as another three horses fell, this time throwing one of the jockeys over the hedge at the side of the track; he rolled along the ground, then stood up, sending the crowd into rapturous applause and cheers.

"He's ok," the commentator said to his colleague.

His colleague just nodded and kept watching his screen. "No, I don't believe it! Two more down!" he said, standing up from his chair, nearly pulling his headphones off his head. He sat back down, adjusting his microphone and trying to compose himself.

The horses carried on thundering up the course, bumping into each other, jostling for pole position. Another jump; "Three more down!" shouted the commentator, jumping from his chair again and knocking his microphone off the desk.

"We have two horses pulling away from the pack," said the other commentator, trying to fill in while his colleague tried to find it under his desk. Unfortunately, in the commotion, he knocked his chair over so when he sat down, he fell to the floor. His legs up in the air, flat on his back, his colleague trying to keep going with the race while fighting back laughter. "So, it's *MARGARETANDROYBOY* and *PERFECT PETER* neck and neck as we come to the last jump."

Suddenly, the crowd fell silent and just stood still, like they had seen a ghost. "What the …?" The commentators looked at their screens and then at the racecourse. They blinked twice and couldn't believe their eyes.

As the horses were running up the racecourse, the grass was disappearing behind them; not a blade was left in sight. No one could believe what they were seeing. All the spectators looked at each other in complete disbelief. What was happening? What was this?

"Don't look behind you, riders, just keep going!" shouted the steward over the Tannoy.

The jockeys all looked behind them to see what was happening. They couldn't believe their eyes — no one had ever seen anything like it. The jockeys just kept going — it now wasn't about winning, it was just about not disappearing with the grass. The steward had opened one of the fences at the side of the course that led to the car park — no chance of concrete disappearing, was there?

When all the jockeys and horses were safely through, the steward closed the fence and looked at the jockeys. "I don't know …?" They all watched as the grass from the whole racecourse completely disappeared, but where? "I'll call the police," said the steward.

"And tell them what?" said one of the jockeys.

This was a question the police couldn't answer. Only a special pair could solve this one …

Sunday April 14*, 2024,
theherald.co.uk - No.20245

Check out the latest
weather on page 14

Grass Stolen at The Grand National!

Police are baffled. The grass was stolen while the horses were running. "It was weird, we all watched as the grass just disappeared, it just went, and I had £50 on *PeterPerfect*," said one spectator.

An offical for the racecourse said, "One minute the grass was there and the next minute it was gone. It was like it was being pulled from underneath the ground."
Police are asking anyone with information to contact them.

The superintendent in charge of the investigation said, "We have no clues or suspects at this time. Why anyone would want to steal the grass from the racecourse while the horses are running or at any other time is beyond me.

By **Abigail Hirst**, Photo **Paul Cutts**

Jake was like any other Jack Russell cross terrier. Well, that was what his owners Coral and Bruce Ward thought. But to his friends and the animals who visited the park every day, Jake and his best friend Sammy, a whippet, were heroes.

"Right, Jake," said Coral. "We're off to work. Be a good boy, see you later."

The kitchen door shut, then Jake heard the front door shut, and then the car moved down the drive. *Finally*, he thought, *time to go to work myself*. Jake pushed against the panel under the cooker to reveal a secret passage and crawled inside. "Wheeeeeeeeeeee!" he yelled as he went down the helter skelter.

"Will you ever get bored of that?" Sammy asked when Jake finally got to the bottom.

"Morning, treacle," Jake replied.

"I've told you, my name is Sammy, and I've no idea why you say that every morning. You're not even from London." Sammy was the brains of the outfit. Jake was clearly not; he was more the muscle. Jake liked it that way — he liked fighting.

"We've got a new assignment coming through. There's been reports of grass going missing all over the country, and HQ wants us to investigate."

"Grass?" Jake looked puzzled.

"Yes, grass, Jake, another weird one. Maybe our weirdest yet. How long have you got before the dog walker comes to take you to the park, Jake?" Sammy asked.

"When the big arm on the clock goes straight up and the little arm goes one to the side of the big arm," Jake said. He wasn't the smart one, remember.

Sammy rolled his eyes. He'd tried to teach Jake how to tell the time but had given up when Jake had got angry and destroyed the clock. "Right," Sammy said, "let's get out there and start questioning our fellow dogs."

Reader, stop!! What am I doing? This is not where the story starts. The story starts at Battersea Dogs and Cats Home about a year or so ago, with Gino …

Gino was a Chihuahua, who despite his size (he was eight inches tall), had already had four homes. Each time, the family had brought him back, and each time, they had said they couldn't cope with his attitude. So, he was back at Battersea Dog and Cats Home awaiting family number five, and hopefully, this time it would be his forever home. His carer, Claire, had high hopes this time. She'd even made him a posh poster for his kennel to make him more appealing to prospective adopters.

BATTERSEA	
Dogs Name:	Gino
Age:	2 Years
Breed:	Chihuahua
Sex:	Dog
Good with Other Dogs:	Just needs time to get to know them
Good with Cats:	No

Additional information – Gino needs a home preferably without children and especially not small children. He needs someone assertive and able to stick to the ground rules of being alpha male / female.

Any questions, please see Claire

Two months passed, but every time someone came to visit Battersea, they completely bypassed Gino. Claire was so upset; she loved this little dog. "They just need to get to know you, Gino," she said one day as family number five walked past his kennel.

*

It was a beautiful summer's day when Phillip's mum and dad decided that today was the day they would bring home a rescue dog. Phillip was a big, grey Great Dane. He was 18 months old, and his mum and dad wanted to get him a friend, someone he could play with while they were either working from home or in the office. So, they put Phillip's lead and harness on and fastened him in the car, then got in themselves. "Right, Phillip, are you ready to pick your new best friend today?" They set off on the 45-minute journey to Battersea. The window was open in the back so Phillip could stick his head out. The wind blew through his jowls, flicking drool all down the side of the car and up into the air. As they passed a cyclist, a large bit of drool landed on his hands, making him veer off the road onto the path and into a laurel hedge.

"Sorry!" Phillip's mum shouted, making sure the cyclist wasn't hurt. "You'd better wind the window up before someone else gets covered."

They arrived at Battersea at 10 a.m., unfastened Phillip, and brought him into the office. Claire was waiting for them.

"You must be Mr and Mrs Fletcher, and you must be Phillip," she said, bending over to pat Phillip, who responded by wagging his whole back end.

"Yes, I'm Natalie, and this is my husband, Mick,"

Natalie said.

"Follow me. I'll take you into our waiting room, then I'll bring the dog I think is a perfect match for you." She led them into the waiting room and then off she went. To get ... who else? Gino.

She wasn't gone five minutes before the door opened and in walked Gino. Phillip stood up, towering over him. His mum looked at her husband. "It's like David and Goliath! I don't think this is a good fit, Claire," she said. "Wait, oh my!" Phillip had laid back down to Gino's level, which meant Gino could reach his head and was licking Phillip's face. Phillip rolled onto his back, at which Gino walked onto his belly. "Phillip actually looks like he's laughing." Claire said she'd never seen Gino play in all the time he'd been with them (on and off) since he was six months old.

"Looks like we've got a winner. I think Phillip's in love," said Natalie, who looked at her husband to see if he was happy for them to take Gino home. Much to her surprise, he was crying.

"Looks like Gino has finally found his forever home," he said, wiping away the tears.

"Amazing!" said Claire. "I'll go and get the adoption forms." She disappeared and came back with what looked like a hundred forms. Natalie and Mick didn't mind as long as Phillip was happy, and clearly, he was.

So, off Gino went to his new home. Phillip's mum and dad watched as both dogs followed each other all over the house and slept together curled up in the same bed. They were just as they'd wanted, best friends. A few days later, it was time for Gino to leave the house, and not just the garden but to go outside on his first proper walk to Regent's Park. Both their leads were clipped onto their collars. Gino took a deep breath as the front door opened; he could see the park across the street. He stepped through the door, down the path, across the street and through the huge gates into the park. He was outside!

Their leads were unclipped, Gino looked at Phillip, Phillip looked at Gino, and they were away.

"Phillip, I'm outside, I'm playing!!" Gino shouted as he spun around so much he became dizzy and fell over. His mum ran over to check he hadn't hurt himself.

"Come on, Gino," Phillip called as he ran towards the middle of the park. Gino got up and ran after him as quickly as his little legs could take him. Don't forget he was only eight inches tall. Phillip was a horse compared to Gino.

Suddenly, Phillip stopped. "I have the other dogs in the park to introduce you to, Gino," he said as a little dog zoomed past them both.

"Hello," said the little dog.

"Wayne, stop, I have some ..." It was too late; the little dog had gone. "That was Wayne. He's a miniature dachshund. All the other dogs in the park walk about three or four miles. Not Wayne, he runs 10 miles even with his little legs, which are smaller than yours!"

Gino looked down at his legs. Phillip was right, of course, they were small, but how could another dog's be even smaller, he wondered as he tried to find Wayne in the park.

"There he is!" shouted Phillip. "Let's try to stop him so you can meet him." Phillip jumped in front of Wayne as he tried to ZOOM past. Poor Wayne went crashing into Phillip, which sent him flying into the air. He landed on his back with his legs still running.

"Hello, I'm Wayne," he said from upside down.

"Wayne, this is Gino. He's my best friend, and this is his first day in the park."

Gino looked at Phillip. He had never been anyone's best friend before.

"Welcome, Gino, it's lovely to meet you. I'm sure we'll see a lot of each other. Sorry, I must go. I have goals I need to reach." Wayne was gone.

Phillip laughed. "That's Wayne," he said, looking around the park for the next character he wanted to introduce Gino to. "Gino, follow me. I want you to meet Charles." Phillip started to walk over to a bench neatly cradling a big oak tree. There sat Charles, a British bulldog, whose owner was sitting on the bench saying hello to everyone, including dogs, who walked past. "Morning, Charles," said Phillip, "I have someone new for you to meet. This is Gino."

"Oh, good morning, Gino. Welcome to Regent's Park," said Charles in a very posh British accent. Charles was clearly an older gentleman. His face was grey, and he looked very distinguished with a Union Jack bandana on. His owner was a middle-aged lady, very well dressed.

"Hello, gentlemen," she said, passing them both a biscuit. "Have you come to say hello to Charles? Charles, isn't that lovely?"

Phillip liked Charles's mum; she always spoke to them like they were human, and more importantly, she had biscuits, and posh biscuits at that. Gino said hello while he finished his biscuit.

"Right, we must go, Charles. Gino has other dogs to meet. See you tomorrow!" Charles saluted. "Charles thinks he was in the army, but we all know he wasn't. Dogs aren't in the army, but we all like Charles, so we play along. His owner adopted him a few years ago. He's quite old and doesn't walk very far, but she spoils him, and rightly so," Phillip said, nodding his head.

Next, Phillip saw the triplets. "Oh, Gino, you're going to love these three, they are so much fun!!"

"Morning, Phillip," the triplets said in unison: Three West Highland white terrier brothers who were full of fun and occasional mischief.

"Morning, Maurice, Barry and Robin, I'd like to introduce you to Gino. This is his first day in the park," Phillip said very proudly, puffing out his chest.

"Hello, Gino, we are very pleased to meet you. Welcome to our beautiful park. I think you'll be very happy here," said Maurice, dropping the ball he was carrying.

"Maurice, Barry, Robin," came a call from across the park, "time to go home."

"That's Mum, sorry, we have to go. See you tomorrow, guys. Hopefully, we can play together soon," said Robin, picking up Maurice's ball and running towards the voice that had called them.

"Their parents are massive Bee Gees fans, so they are named after them," said Phillip, walking towards another dog he wanted to introduce Gino to.

What's a Bee Gee? Gino thought but didn't say out loud — he didn't want to seem ignorant.

"Morning, Wolfgang. Gino, I'd like to introduce Wolfgang. He's a German wirehaired pointer. If you lose anything, Wolfgang is the dog to find it. Wolfgang, this is Gino," Phillip said.

"Hello, Gino. Phillip told me yesterday you're finally coming out. I'm so happy for you!" Wolfgang sat down so as not to tower over Gino. The other dogs Gino had met today were little dogs. Wolfgang, on the other hand, was big. Gino liked the big dog's beard and was a little jealous he couldn't grow one of his own. "Gino, have you met Laura yet?" Wolfgang asked.

"Laura?" Gino looked at Phillip, a little puzzled.

"No, but we're going to meet her now," said Phillip. "See you later, Wolfgang." They said their goodbyes, "I've saved the best till last," said Phillip.

Phillip started to run over to some bushes way over on the left-hand side of the park, and Gino followed. "Where are we going?" said Gino, very out of breath.

"I have a friend who lives under these bushes. I bring her biscuits every day!" Phillip shouted back; he was way ahead by now. Sure enough, Gino could see a small dog hiding under the bushes. "Morning, Laura," Phillip said, dropping the biscuits he'd hidden in his harness down onto the ground for her.

"Morning, Phillip, and you must be Gino." Laura winked as she looked him up and down, sizing him up.

"Laura's a stray. Her mum was taken into care about a year ago and no one came to get her. When the council cleared the house, she ran into the park, and she's been here ever since. I bring biscuits and other bits when I can." Gino could tell that in her day she had been a beautiful dog but now, living outdoors, her hair was dirty and knotted.

"I'm an apricot poodle," said Laura. "My mum was my best friend. We did everything together." A tear came into her eye as she remembered her past life. "But I'm here now living free," her voice lifting at the end of the sentence like she was declaring how fabulous her life was to anyone that was nearby and listening.

"Gino, Phillip, where are you?"

"Mum's shouting at us. See you tomorrow, Laura, be

safe," said Phillip, licking her on the forehead.

"Nice to meet you, Gino," Laura said, winking again.

"I like her," Gino said as they walked back across the park.

"Teatime, you two," Mum announced, clapping her hands as they both ran back to her. "Did you enjoy your first outing?" she said, giving him a big hug. Gino wanted to tell her how happy he was and that he'd never been so happy in his short life. He licked her cheek instead, which did the trick because she hugged him tighter.

Life was pretty perfect for the Fletcher family. Gino and Phillip were inseparable. There were walks to the park, the seaside, Airbnb's. This was about to change, not in a bad way, but life for Gino and Phillip was about to get a little bit more exciting.

4

Gino and Phillip were ready for their usual walk in the park, same as every day, nothing different there. They crossed the road, walked through the park gates, Mum unclipped their leads, and they were off, straight over to Laura, nothing unusual there either, but no Laura. "Where is she?" Phillip started looking under all the bushes. "She's not here, Gino! Look over there in the thicker bushes; you can fit." Phillip was starting to panic now. Gino started hunting, but still no Laura.

"Are you looking for Laura, mate?" Gino looked around but could see no one. "Down here, governor," came the voice again.

Gino looked down to see a little brown mouse staring at him. "Did you say something?" said Gino, a little puzzled.

"Yes, I know where Laura is. Get your friend and follow me."

"Phillip!" shouted Gino, scrabbling out of the thick undergrowth.

Phillip came bounding over. "Have you found her?" he asked.

"Maybe — we need to follow that mouse." Gino looked over to the mouse and then to his friend.

"Mouse?" Phillip was confused about what was going on.

They both followed the mouse for what seemed like miles. Well, it was to Gino; he only had little legs.

Suddenly the mouse stopped. "She's in there."

In front of them was a rundown shed at the far end of the park, away from the public part. Phillip pushed the door open, and Gino followed. There were no windows in the shed, so the only light coming in was the light from the open door. Phillip and Gino stood still, waiting for their eyes to adjust to the low light. It only took a few moments, but Gino stuck to Phillip's side until he could see there was no danger.

"Laura!" Phillip shouted, "You ok?"

"I'm fine, Phillip. Thank you for coming. I need to explain why I'm here." Laura took a deep breath. "Right, don't interrupt me, either of you; I've got a lot to tell you both."

Phillip and Gino just nodded. They respected Laura and knew she was tough.

"This is Donald. He's a London Underground mouse. Unfortunately, builders have decided to update some of the old disused stations and tracks, which means that hundreds of mouse families will become homeless when they rip out all the unwanted bits that have been added since they were built originally. They don't have much time. We've seen them measuring and moving things already. It's awful — where will they go?"

"Let me have a think about it and ask around," Phillip said, turning towards the door. "Come on, Gino, we need to get back or Mum will wonder where we are."

Gino followed. "What will we do?" he asked as they crossed the park back towards Mum, who was shouting their names very loudly.

"There you are. I was getting worried," she said, clipping their leads back on their collars. They made their way back home. Phillip was very quiet. Gino left him alone; he was clearly thinking.

After tea, their dad suddenly got off the sofa and said, "I fancy a pint, Phillip, do you want to accompany me?"

Phillip stood up. Of course he wanted to go to the pub;

he might find an answer there. Gino didn't like being at the pub; it was far too loud for him. His mum and dad thought maybe something had happened to him in one of his past homes because he howled from start to finish. Not relaxing at all and very upsetting to put him through, so he stayed at home to look after Mum. Dad said he was the man of the house while his dad was out.

Phillip and his dad made the 10-minute walk to the local. The Roundhouse was a thin pub, nestled in between two houses, with tiled floors and stained-glass windows with flowers and butterflies on them. On the outside, the hanging baskets were so big and so full of petunias, ivy, fuchsias and begonias, they looked like they would pull the brackets off the walls. They walked into the pub, which had a small bar and three tables at the front, where Phillip could see two dogs lying on the floor, not the dog he was looking for. Then a long corridor on the left led to small snug rooms, each with two tables in. Mick bought his pint, then made his way down the corridor to find an empty snug room where he could enjoy his pint in peace. Phillip, on the other hand, or should I say paw, had other ideas; he was looking for someone.

Suddenly, Phillip pulled his dad into one of the snugs. He'd found the dog he was looking for, Hamish. Hamish was a guide dog. Phillip always bowed his head when he saw him as did all the other dogs. Guide dogs are classed as the highest of high in the dog world and quite rightly so; they are heroes. "We need to have a chat if you are staying for another?" he said.

"I think we are here for the night, Phillip, so what can I do for you?" Hamish said, lying down next to Phillip.

Phillip explained about the mice's situation and that a

home needed to be found very soon. "Do you know of anywhere? I know you go to the zoo a lot. Do you think there could be somewhere for them there? We need tunnels and safety, of course, somewhere they won't be disturbed again," Phillip said.

Hamish thought for a while and then said, "I might know someone, or should I say a few someones, who could help us," at which Hamish's owner stood up.

"Goodnight," he said, grabbing Hamish's harness.

"Back to work," Hamish said, standing up and turning back into a guide dog.

Phillip watched as Hamish left the snug room. He was in awe of him, and hopefully, Hamish could help the mice.

Phillip went back home to Gino and explained he'd met Hamish, who was going to ask at the zoo if there were anywhere the mice could go. They would let Laura know in the morning that someone was on the case and cross all their paws something would turn up.

Phillip and Gino didn't sleep a wink; they tossed and turned all night worrying about Hamish and if he would have a plan, or his contact at the zoo would come through. When dawn came, Phillip and Gino plagued their mum to go out.

"My, you two are giddy this morning! Wait a minute and I'll get your leads," she said, nearly falling over Gino. Well, she couldn't really fall over Phillip now, could she? As soon as their leads were on, she opened the front door, and they were off. They were like huskies as they sped over the zebra crossing, bumping into a lady pushing a baby buggy.

"Sorry, I don't know what's wrong with them! I think they've heard it's free biscuit day at the park," she said as they sped past.

All the lady saw was a blur of dogs. "Doggy," the baby gurgled. These two dogs weren't meant to be stroked today.

As soon as the leads were unclipped, they both ran off towards the bushes to find Laura, and hopefully, Donald. They found Laura curled up under a bush, and as soon as she saw them, she stood up.

"Do you two have good news?" Her eyes were wide open with excitement.

"No, but we do have Hamish. He's going to the zoo today, and he's going to ask around. Hopefully, he'll have news later in the week. In the meantime, I think we should go to the Underground tunnels and see if we can find somewhere else for the mice to live." Phillip seemed really keen on this plan, Gino not so much, as the Underground was dark and dirty. So he'd heard, anyway; not somewhere he fancied going to. "We'll sneak out tonight when everyone has gone to bed. Laura, you meet us at the park gates at 11 p.m." Laura agreed, and they ran back to where Natalie was sitting.

"What have you just done, Phillip? We can't go into the Underground, especially at night!" Gino had a touch of fear in his voice.

"Don't worry, Gino, it'll be fine. There's nothing scary in the tunnels. Nothing can hurt us," Phillip said. The words came out of his mouth, but he didn't believe them. He just wanted to show Laura he was brave, nothing else.

"Right, come on, you two, I have to go work. Let's go home." At that, their leads were clipped, and they started back across the park and home.

On the other side of the park, Hamish was guiding his

owner to the zoo. They went at least once a week, and to be fair, it was Hamish's favourite outing. He got to be Super Dog. He would hold his head up high, and people would look at him in awe. Other mere mortal dogs were not allowed in the zoo, so people noticed. He was very proud to be a guide dog. They arrived at the gates.

"Morning, you two. We've had baby meerkats since you came last week. I know how much you love the meerkats," the lady in the kiosk said, popping chewing gum in between each word. "Go through and have a lovely day," she said, lifted the gate, and popped again.

"We'll go straight to the meerkats, Hamish, if that's ok," his owner said.

Hamish knew, actually, where he was going. His owner loved to listen to the meerkats digging and running around. It was all about animals who were busy and made lots of noise for him. Hamish knew that the meerkats heard and saw everything, so they might know of somewhere the mice could go. It was only a 10-minute walk to the meerkat enclosure, so when they got there, Hamish stopped near the wall which ran around the whole enclosure. Every metre or so, there was a Perspex viewing window so little children could see the meerkats without climbing on the wall. Hamish thought they had him in mind when they put them in; they were a perfect height, and he could watch as the meerkats played.

"Oy! Meerkat, I need to ask you a question."

One of the meerkats, maybe the head one, came over. "Yes, dog?" he answered.

Hamish explained about the mice, London Underground, new home, builders, remodelling — if you ask me, he went on far too long. The meerkat listened and listened and then moved about because he had a cramp and then listened some more. When Hamish finally finished, the meerkat said, "Right, leave it with me. I'll ask around." Then off he went down his burrow.

10.30 p.m. finally came. Mick and Natalie said goodnight to the boys and went to bed.

"I didn't think they would ever go," Phillip said, looking at Gino, who unfortunately looked scared to death at the thought of going into the London Underground at night. They clipped their night lights on their collars and climbed into their high viz jackets — no mean feat when you don't have thumbs.

Phillip had hidden his dad's torch under his blanket when they got back earlier. "Laura can hold this because she hasn't got a night light for her collar or a high viz," Phillip said, ever the planner. They both sneaked out of the house, careful not to wake their parents, crossed the road and ran into the park, two dogs on a mission.

"Laura, are you ok? Here, I have this torch."

Laura took hold of the torch in her mouth and followed the two dogs over to the far side of the park to the Underground entrance. Even though all the gates were now locked, they were small enough to get through the gaps in the gates. All three of them had never been here. It was very eerie, and Gino didn't like it. The shadows Laura's torch was making all looked like monsters, dog-eating monsters, maybe!!!

"Phillip," said Gino, "are there any monsters down here?"

"No, just rats and mice," Laura said, trying to make him feel better, but it didn't work; all he could then think of was rats as big as cows roaming the Underground in search of unsuspecting victims. He could see the newspaper headline now:

TWO DOGS MISSING. LAST SEEN AT HOME.
OWNERS ARE COMPLETELY BAFFLED AS TO
WHERE THEY WENT!!!

Gino, he thought, *get a hold of yourself.*

They walked through the unused tunnels Donald had told them about. He was right, they were beautiful. They could see all the builders' machinery and tools.

"This is a huge job," Phillip said. "I think we might have longer than we thought to find Donald and his friends and family a new home." Phillip hoped more than he actually knew, but he was right — renovation does take longer than building new. His mum watched tonnes of programmes on TV about it. They had walked through an old station which was in full re-modelling mode and onto a station that was being used.

"It's probably best we don't go any further. This is a busy station and no use for Donald," said Phillip, a little relieved himself they were calling it a day, sorry, night.

Gino couldn't wait to get out of there. He definitely didn't need to be told twice they were going home. They walked back the way they came a little quicker than on the way there, all three wanting to get back to their beds, even Laura, who slept outside. When they reached the park and safety, they said their goodbyes and went their separate ways. Unfortunately, the whole experience was useless; it had not accomplished anything other than to scare the group. None of them ever spoke of that night again. It was a learning curve and now it was done.

Over the next few days, Phillip paced all over the house, he paced around the garden, he paced up and down and around the park. To say he didn't wait patiently for an answer was an understatement.

Natalie said after the third day, "What's up with Phillip? He's been pacing up and down for three days now. Are you going to the pub to watch the footie? Maybe you should take him with you. The change of scenery may do him good."

Mick grunted and grabbed Phillip's lead.

"I hope Hamish has an answer, Phillip," Gino said, watching Phillip walk through the open door.

Together, they walked down the street towards the pub. Phillip hoped Hamish would be there; he didn't even know if the mice had found a new home. If not, he'd have to think of something else, but what? They walked into the pub, and phew, Hamish was already there.

"Hi, Phillip, I have news. You'll be happy!" said Hamish. "I'll be in the third snug," he said, leading his owner off down the corridor.

"Pint, please," said Mick to the lady behind the bar.

"£6.40, please," she replied.

Mick grabbed his pint and started down the corridor. Phillip pulled him into the third snug as instructed by Hamish.

"Right, Phillip, the meerkats have a solution. They think they can dig under their enclosure to the Underground into the tunnels. The mice only need small holes at the other end to get in, so no one will see them and suspect what lies behind." Hamish took a breath. "They will start straight away as they know this is urgent. The meerkats overheard their keepers talking about parts of the Underground being closed for refurbishments. I think we have around two months before the mice will be homeless." At that, Hamish finished his story.

"Tell them to go ahead, Hamish. I will tell Laura and

she can tell the mice. The mice can help from the other end, and hopefully, it won't be long before they meet in the middle." Phillip was so happy. He couldn't wait to tell Gino, Laura, and of course, more importantly, the mice.

Mick watched the footie while Phillip and Hamish talked about digging, mice and whether Phillip should ask Laura on a date. This topic made Phillip uncomfortable, and he was more than happy to change the subject and get back to digging.

After his second pint and a very disappointing 2-0 defeat for his team, Mick walked back home rather slowly and with his head down. Phillip, on the other hand, was so excited with his news, he tried to hurry the walk up.

"Phillip, stop pulling! You don't understand what's just happened. We may as well have stayed at home, we were awful!" Mick said, stopping in the street and sighing.

Phillip didn't understand football. All he knew was that their plan to find a new home for the mice was in motion; they wouldn't be homeless after all. When Phillip got home, he was bursting to tell Gino what had happened. "Gino, Gino, come quick!" he yelled. Gino jumped out of bed and ran over to Phillip. "I've got so much to tell you, Gino. It's the most amazing news," he said, trying to catch his breath.

"Slow down Phillip! You'll pass out! Start from the beginning," Gino said, licking Phillip's paw. Being so little, it was the only part he could reach. Phillip took a breath and started at the beginning. This was going to be a long story, so reader, if you fancy a cup of tea, I'd make one now.

The meerkats had already started digging their tunnels. They would dig under the zoo to the Underground, to a disused station, and then they would also dig sideways from their enclosure under the giraffes, who had a huge field, perfect for so many little rodents. They could eat the grass on an evening when the zoo was closed and the giraffes had gone to bed.

This was going to be a big job, Donald thought. One day, after waiting eight hours in the old station, he'd counted all the beautiful Victorian tiles which lined the walls. He counted how many rivets the tracks had, and now he was counting the sleepers holding the tracks off the gravel floor.

"Hi, Donald." Laura was here, and she'd brought some cheese and fruit. Only a small amount — mice don't eat much — but she thought he might like some company. "Any movement yet? Can you see anything?" she asked him, hoping for something. The poor mouse had been pacing the station for days now. They both knew it was a big job. Donald shook his head. "Never mind, let's have a chat and a little bit of a snack." They sat side by side, and Laura broke a little cheese off the wedge and put it down on the ground along with a grape. Maybe too much, but he'd been pacing, and he'd probably worked up quite an appetite. Laura thought it would be nice to talk about something other than the tunnel. "So, how's the family, Donald? Are they all keeping well?" Laura asked.

"Yes, thanks, Laura, they are all good. We've packed our suitcases ready for the new move," Donald said, looking at the crack in the wall again.

Well, that didn't work, Laura thought to herself. All of a sudden, they both heard something. They turned to the wall and saw dirt falling through the crack and then … a head.

"Hello," said the meerkat, "nice to see you both. Have you sat there long?"

Donald ran over to the meerkat, who was, as you can imagine, filthy. "I could hug you," Donald shouted. He was quite emotional.

"Right, what do we do now?" Laura asked.

The meerkat looked down at Donald. "Go and get all the mice. We need their help digging the tunnels to the giraffes. You might as well help; it is your new home, after all."

Donald didn't need to be asked twice. He ran off towards the station where they were currently living. "Thank you!" he shouted as he ran off.

"Is there anything I could do, Mr Meerkat? What is your name?" Laura asked.

"My name is Ian, and I'd love a cup of tea, no sugar or milk," the meerkat replied.

Laura hadn't expected that response, but she was happy to go on the hunt for a cuppa. She unfortunately had no idea where to get one.

"Everyone!" Donald shouted, "The meerkat has dug through. We can go into the tunnels and start digging under the giraffes' enclosure."

"Hooray!" Everyone cheered. If anyone had been listening, they would have heard the smallest squeak in history, but to the mice, it was a huge cheer. The mice gathered all their belongings and started to follow Donald. None of them had ever been to these new tunnels, so they followed very closely. It was only a short distance from their old home to the new tunnel, but they had tiny legs, so it was a long walk, and the baby mice climbed onto their mothers' backs when they got tired.

Donald had done this journey a few times over the last few days, but he knew the other mice needed a rest. "Shall we rest?" he shouted back.

"No, let's just get there," everyone said back.

Donald kept pressing on. It was him who needed the break. He'd had cheese and a grape — not good to be running on a full stomach.

Donald saw Laura ahead. The mice had been so long that the tea she'd finally found had been drunk, and the meerkat was now having a nap.

"Donald, hello. Everyone, it's so nice to see you all. Ian, wake up."

Ian woke to hundreds of mice all staring at him. "Hello," Ian said, "follow me." Ian crawled through the crack in the tiles, and the mice eagerly followed. The tunnel was dark and dirty, and the baby mice were scared. They clung to their mothers, shaking with fear and cold.

"It'll be over soon," said one of the mothers, trying not to sound scared.

"Right, we'll stay here for the night. This is our enclosure," said Ian. "We've collected some grass, and Laura's given us some cheese. It'll be very cramped, but it's only for tonight. You'll be in your new home in the morning." He was right; it was very cramped. There were feet and tails everywhere, and no one really slept. But it was only for one night. They could all pull together, and in the morning, they'd be in their new home, and they could rest peacefully with no fear of trains, builders or architects.

Morning came, but not quickly enough if you asked the meerkats. Ian was already up, mostly because he wanted his home back, but also because he liked these little mice, and a promise is a promise. "Right, mice, we have a surprise for you. We've already dug your new home — are you ready to see it?" Ian asked. Donald couldn't believe his ears. He saw little heads bobbing up and down. Ian continued, "We've been busy. You've got about 10 little nests off five tunnels. I hope you like it." Ian took a deep breath. He was very proud of what the meerkats had achieved.

The mice followed Ian.

"Visit anytime," one of the other meerkats said as the last mouse went into the tunnel.

"I'll miss them," another said with a tear in his eye.

The tunnels opened into little side tunnels, then at the end there were nests all prepared with straw and grass.

"We're going to be very happy here, thank you, Ian," Donald said.

"Visit whenever you want," said Ian. "The opening to the field is just over there where you can see light. Just be careful, only go up at dusk, and watch out for owls." At that, Ian went back through the tunnel.

"What a lovely meerkat," Donald said. "We all must thank Laura, Phillip and Gino. I'll find them tomorrow." It was now time to unpack and get settled in — home sweet home.

5

Donald awoke very early; he was desperate to see Gino, Phillip and Laura to thank them for helping him move into his new home. He ran through the meerkat enclosure, careful not to wake anyone. They had all had a busy few days and probably needed their sleep. He ran through the tunnels leading to the railway station, and on his way, noticed a large opening on his left which looked like an old office, maybe for the station master back in the day. He crawled through the little opening onto the station and ran along the tracks so the builders, if they were working, didn't see him. He only had little legs, so this journey would take a while. He hoped he hadn't missed them at the park; he hoped that he had got up early enough. He ran up the stairs to the surface, admiring the tiles on the walls. They were beautiful; all the greens were so vibrant. *Victorians knew how to decorate,* he thought. *Must press on.* When he finally got to the top, he could see the sun had just started to rise. He had got up early enough, phew. Wow, the sunrise was beautiful this morning. He took the new day in and ran towards the park.

Gino and Phillip were ready for their walk, their leads were securely fastened, the front door was open, and it was time to go and explore.

"Let's find Laura first," Phillip said, licking Gino's head.

Gino nodded. "I hope Donald is alright," he added, striding through the door. Poor little Gino, having to do ten steps for every one that Phillip did. They crossed the road and entered the park, Natalie unclipped their leads, and they were off straight across the park to where Laura slept.

"Laura!" Phillip shouted as they got near.

"Morning, gentlemen. Look who got up really early to see you."

"Donald!!!" Gino exclaimed, "Are you in your new home? More importantly, is it comfortable?"

"It's amazing, thank you so much! All my family and friends are safe and warm, and we have friends nearby to help us," Donald said with a tear in his eye. "You are the best of the best! You deserve a medal for helping us." Donald now had two tears rolling down his face.

"You are very welcome, Donald. It was our pleasure, and you definitely deserve it. I hope one day we can come to visit," Phillip said, not really thinking about what he was saying. He was just happy they would all be settled and safe.

Just then they heard "Pssst, I hear you help animals who are in distress." A voice seemed to be speaking from the bushes.

"Who said that?" Gino said, trying to see who was speaking to them.

"I did."

This time, they heard movement, and slowly, a squirrel crawled from under the rhododendrons. "Me name's Terry, and I've lost me nuts," he said, flicking his tail and sitting on his back legs. "I buried them around the park, and now I can't find them. Can you help me?" he said, staring straight at Gino, who was about his height. He would have a neck ache trying to look up at Phillip. "You are heroes for helping Donald and his family. I need nuts to feed my family. Without them, we'll go hungry through the summer." He had clasped his little paws together.

"Did you not draw a map so you knew where you'd

buried them?" asked Gino, thinking that would have definitely helped.

"No, never needed a map before, but I'm getting older and the memory's not what it used to be," he said, looking a little embarrassed.

"Sorry, Terry, we didn't mean to upset you. We'll help you," said Phillip, glaring at Gino for clearly saying the wrong thing.

"Right, where do we start? How do we start?" said an excited Laura. Being Gino and Phillip's friend had become so much fun.

"Right," said Terry, "I normally bury them at the bottom of big trees. This park has an awful lot," he said, a little downhearted.

"We may never find them. We will just need to split up," said Gino. "Donald, do you want to help?"

"How can I be of service?" Donald asked eagerly.

"Right, Donald, go and tell Wayne."

Donald saluted and ran off towards Wayne to spread the word.

"Gino, you go north. Laura, you coordinate from here. I'll go west, Terry east," Phillip said, feeling quite bossy but in a good way.

When Donald finally got Wayne's attention, he caught his breath and said, "Wayne, we need your help. Terry the squirrel has buried his nuts and he's forgotten where he buried them. He knows they are under the biggest trees, but that's all. Can you help spread the word to the other dogs in the park? They need to dig under the trees, find the nuts and take them to Laura under the rhododendrons over there." Donald pointed to the far side of the park.

Before Donald finished pointing, Wayne was off. He

ran across the park to Charles. "Morning, Charles," said Wayne, "we need your help." Wayne went on to explain the Terry predicament.

"Happy to help the little chap," said Charles, breathing in to make his huge chest even bigger. "When you're a soldier, you help everyone, no matter what," Charles said, saluting Wayne.

"Thank you, Charles. Sorry I can't stop; I must spread the word."

The next dogs were the triplets: Maurice, Robin and Barry.

"Morning, gentlemen, I have a competition for you." Wayne explained the problem again, this time telling the triplets there was a prize at the end for the dog who collected the most nuts. He would fill Laura in so she could think of a prize at the end that would definitely spur the triplets on. Of course, they were very happy to help, and to beat their brothers at the same time was even better.

Next, Wolfgang, who loved to find things — anything. Every dog Wayne spoke to knew of Phillip and Gino's good deed, so were happy to help. Who would think a dog digging under a tree was suspicious?

Gino ran across the park until he came to a big tree. Maybe he could smell the nut under the ground. He placed his nose to the dirt and started to sniff, but unfortunately, all he got was a nose full of dirt. *No*, he thought, *start digging. At least they won't be too deep.* He moved the leaves first and started to dig, just the topsoil. He didn't need to dig to Australia. Nothing, so he moved around the tree and started to dig again. *What's this? Yippee! An acorn.* He'd found his first, hopefully, of many nuts. He gently picked it up in his mouth and ran back across the park, dropping it under the rhododendron bush, where Laura was waiting to keep an eye on the nuts and to let the others know which trees had been dug under. He couldn't believe there were at least 10 others there already. "Fantastic!" he shouted.

Laura explained the competition Wayne had got the triplets involved in.

"Well done, Wayne, quick thinking," he said as he ran back across the park. "This is fun!" he yelled as he passed Phillip running back to Laura. He ran to the next tree and started to dig.

While this was going on, the gardeners in the park had stopped what they were doing and were all watching the dogs and a squirrel running back and forth digging under trees, collecting acorns and running across the park. They all looked at each other and sat down on a bench scratching their heads. "What do you think is going on?" one said to another.

"I have no idea; do you think their owners have trained them to look for treasure?"

"Maybe, but that doesn't explain the squirrel. He's doing it as well."

The gardeners were puzzled and gave up weeding to watch this weird but fun spectacle. "Maybe it'll become clear as we watch. Coffee?" one said, opening his flask and pouring what looked more like treacle than coffee.

"Yes, please. I have custard creams if you want to dunk?" The gardeners settled in to watch the show. This was more exciting than their usual day in the park.

The triplets were finding the most, and Laura had such a pile by now, she was still thinking of what a prize could be when the answer landed in front of her. Poor Wayne had found not a single nut, but he'd found all the missing dog toys from probably years ago. He was so proud that she didn't have the heart to tell him he'd found the wrong things. The dogs and the squirrel kept running, digging and finding for about an hour.

Natalie and the other owners had now joined the gardeners on the bench to watch the show. Natalie was working from home today, so she could clock on whenever. This was much more fun.

Under the bush, the pile of nuts was huge. Laura had made sure the triplets had exactly the same amount so all three would get a prize. Otherwise, they would fall out, and that argument could last for months. It wasn't worth it. She looked at the pile and thought Terry could feed his family for two or three years, never mind through the summer. Phillip was now thinking they may have found another squirrel's hoard, but he was sure Terry would share.

The gardeners had been sitting so long, they'd run out of coffee and biscuits. "Bet David Attenborough's never seen this behaviour," one said to the other. "We should have filmed it and sent it to him."

Wayne ran around the park to let all the dogs know to stop collecting and meet under the bush with Gino, Phillip and Laura. The triplets were back first. They wanted to know who'd won the competition. Then Wayne and Wolfgang came back, closely followed by Donald. Poor Charles was last; he couldn't run very fast, and he'd only collected two nuts. Laura moved some from the other piles onto his; he was an officer, after all.

"Wow," said Terry when he saw how many nuts had been collected.

"I must get back. The other mice will be awake now and wondering where I've got to," said Donald.

"Thank you, Donald. You are the biggest-hearted mouse I've ever met," said Terry, wanting to give Donald a hug but deciding against it. "I can't thank you all enough," said Terry with a little tear in his eye. "I need to bury them …" He was stopped mid-sentence by Phillip.

"NOOOOOOOOO! Don't bury them. We CAN'T do that again."

All the dogs started to giggle. It had been hard work finding the nuts, but they had all enjoyed their walk this morning — something different to a normal day.

"Who won?" shouted the triplets.

"Well," said Laura, "It was a three-way tie between you three, so you get to pick your prize from the toys Wayne kindly provided us today."

The triplets looked at each other, then at the pile of toys. "Amazing," they all said and started digging into the hoard. They each picked a toy and happily ran back across the park to their owners, who were still sitting on the bench trying to figure out what had just happened.

"You should do this for a living," said Charles.

"Do what?" said Phillip.

"Help animals. I'm sure there are more out there that need your help." Charles saluted. He'd had a really good time. "This has been the best morning I've had since leaving the army. Thank you for including me," he said as he walked back over to his owner.

"Do you think he's right, there are other animals that need our help?" Gino said.

"Maybe," said Phillip, "but how would we help them? We're just dogs!"

"Tell that to Donald and Terry. You've just become heroes in their eyes," Laura said. She was right, of course; she was always right.

"Gino, Phillip!" shouted their mum, "Time to go home. I think we've all had enough fun for one day." She said her goodbyes to the gardeners and dog owners, who also needed to get back to work. Natalie clipped their leads back onto their collars, completely baffled as to what she had just witnessed. "What were you both doing? Dad's never going to believe me when I tell him tonight!" she said, knowing full well she would never get any answers from these two.

When Mick came home, his wife had a lot to tell him. "Hi, have you had a good day?" he said as he walked into the house. Of course, he was not speaking to his wife but to Gino and Phillip, who greeted him with very waggy tails.

"I've got something to tell you!" his wife shouted from the kitchen. "Come in here when you've taken your shoes and coat off. You won't believe what happened today."

Mick took off his coat and shoes and made his way into the kitchen. He was about to hear the tallest tale of his life. Little did he know, it was completely true, and in the not-so-distant future, things were going to get stranger and a lot weirder.

6

Phillip didn't sleep very well. He was mulling over what the bulldog had said. First they had found Donald and his family a new home, then found Terry's nuts. Were there others out there that needed help? Their help? "Gino, are you asleep?" he asked. Gino was snoring, so maybe that was a yes. He said it a little louder this time.

"I am a big dog!" Gino shouted so loud, Phillip worried that Mum and Dad would hear the bark from upstairs.

"Shhh," Phillip said, checking Mum and Dad weren't moving about. "Gino, I think we need to set up an agency to help other animals like Donald and Terry. I'm sure there must be more like them. I wonder if Laura would like to work with us as well? She's smart enough."

Gino yawned. "Can we sort it in the morning? I'm tired." He curled up in his bed and started to snore again.

Phillip tried to sleep, but he was so excited about talking to Laura and starting the agency. He had so many ideas. Hopefully, Laura would be excited and want to help set it up. He finally dozed off about two hours later, but unfortunately, it was already morning.

"Morning, guys," said Mum as she walked down the stairs. "Who were you barking at last night, Gino? Was it that squirrel from yesterday?" She kissed them both as she passed to go into the kitchen.

"Still don't believe you — as if dogs and a squirrel were digging up nuts," Mick said, still finding the whole story hilarious.

They all had breakfast together, but Phillip wasn't hungry. He was still thinking about what Charles had said.

"Are you feeling unwell, Phillip? It's not like you to leave your breakfast," his mum said, feeling his forehead like a mother would with a child.

Phillip just wanted to get out into the park. He ran to the door barking.

"I know, I'm coming; I just need to get my coat and shoes on."

Phillip ran back to her, then to the door, barking again.

"What's up with him?" said Mick. "He really wants to get out there. Do you think he's got a girlfriend?"

Natalie quickly got ready and clipped their leads on.

"Gino, I'll explain when we find Laura. I don't want to repeat myself, but I've had an idea," Phillip said, running out of the door and nearly pulling his mum over.

"Phillip!" she yelled. "Slow down!"

They walked through the gates into the park, and as soon as their leads were unclipped, they ran off across to where Laura slept under the rhododendrons.

"Laura!" Phillip shouted.

"Good morning, gents, did you sleep well?" she asked.

Phillip was frantic; he had so many ideas, he was bursting to tell them both.

"Phillip, breathe, what's happened?" Laura said, trying to calm him down.

"Right, I've had an amazing idea, so I'll start at the beginning."

They all sat down under the bushes, and Phillip began. "I think we should start an agency to help animals like Terry and Donald with their dilemmas. We did such a good job; There are animals out there that need us. Laura, I'd like you to run the office. You are the most organised dog I've ever met. We are a team, and we should stick together. We just need a place to set up shop." Phillip stopped and looked at their faces. He couldn't quite work out whether they were up for this or even taking it in.

Just then, Donald joined the party. He'd heard some of the pitch. "I know exactly where you can set up shop. I saw a huge open space in the tunnels on the way to the zoo. It's perfect, and Laura can live down there safe and dry." Donald looked very pleased with himself; he could never repay them for their kindness, but hopefully, this would go some way to showing them how grateful he was. "Follow me," he said, pointing across the park.

"Maybe I should carry you, Donald," Phillip said, picking Donald up.

"That tickles," Donald said, laughing.

They all ran towards the tunnels Donald used to get to the zoo. It wasn't long before Donald pointed left. "Just here" he said. They crawled through a small opening which was perfect because you would never know it was there unless you knew it was there. The small gap opened up to a huge cavern. It had electricity points from when it was a signalman's room.

"Donald, this is amazing! Well done," Laura said, kissing Donald on the head.

He immediately blushed and turned away so no one could see.

"We'll set up here. Laura, this is your new home. Everyone, today is the first day of our secret agency, and this is HQ," Phillip said, taking a big deep breath. They all knew they had some hard work ahead, but they acknowledged that helping their fellow animals would be their reward.

They could never have known this humble beginning would eventually lead to a global operation that would help solve one of the greatest mysteries of recent times.

But let's not get ahead of ourselves, that's for later … much later.

Meanwhile, reader, it's maybe time to meet the real heroes of our story …

7

Our unlikely hero number 1 — Jake — had found himself back at the rescue home for the third time. He was only 15 months old. No one could cope with his temper, and unfortunately, he had a dreadful temper. Two people had adopted him, and two people had brought him back. The dog rescue centre he'd been taken back to this time tried to show him in a better light, which wasn't easy.

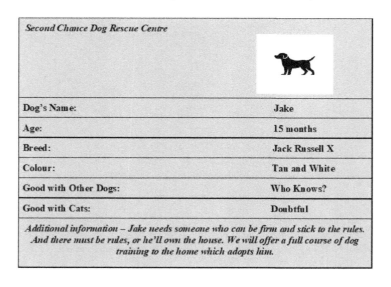

Second Chance Dog Rescue Centre	
Dog's Name:	Jake
Age:	15 months
Breed:	Jack Russell X
Colour:	Tan and White
Good with Other Dogs:	Who Knows?
Good with Cats:	Doubtful

Additional information – Jake needs someone who can be firm and stick to the rules. And there must be rules, or he'll own the house. We will offer a full course of dog training to the home which adopts him.

Jake had no takers. He stayed at the home for three months; no one was willing to give him a new home. That was until Bruce and Coral Ward came to the home. They were looking for a scruffy terrier with a personality and maybe a bit of naughtiness. They looked in every kennel and nothing seemed to fit. Then Coral stopped, she looked at Bruce, and then grabbed his hand and gave it a little squeeze. She'd stopped outside Jake's kennel.

"He's the one," she said, tears rolling down her face.

Bruce looked inside the kennel. Could this be the dog of their dreams? He was perfect; he was everything they had in mind.

"He's a bit of a terror, I'd better warn you. He'll take work and rules," the Warden said. "We offer a dog training course to help you, so you won't do this alone."

Coral had made up her mind. "I'm in love," she said, wiping the tears from her cheek. "What happens now?" she asked. They'd never done this before. Did they need to sign anything?

"We have some forms to fill in, and we need to transfer his medical insurance and ID chip information," said the warden, bringing out what seemed like a hundred forms.

Bruce and Coral were ready to fill in any number of forms to take Jake home; they just knew this was right.

"Right, he's yours," the warden said after the last form was complete.

Bruce looked at his wife, who was crying again. "Looks like we've adopted a dog," he said, passing her another tissue.

Jake was ready and waiting for them with a volunteer holding onto his lead, ready to pass him over, hopefully for the last time.

It was only a 30-minute journey from the dog home to Jake's new home. They hoped that Jake wouldn't feel sick on the journey. Actually, he quite enjoyed it. He was excited to see where he was going to live. He decided he would try harder to be a good and less troublesome terrier, if that was possible. Unfortunately, that didn't go so well, to start with, anyway. Maybe he just needed time to settle in, fingers crossed.

The first instance involved a carrier bag which blew into the garden. Jake saw it land. *What was it*? *Never mind, it didn't matter, it had to DIE*. He crept up the garden in stealth mode, making sure the object hadn't seen or heard him. Pounce! Jake landed straight on top of it, but unfortunately, it was slippery. Jake flew across the garden, hitting the fence, which made him even angrier. He then grabbed the carrier bag, shaking it from side to side, spraying bits of plastic all over the garden. Jake – 1, object – 0. Jake walked back into the house, his head held high. "It won't be messing with me again," he said.

The second instance involved the postman, poor postman. The postman made his way around the street just like every other day, but this day, Jake was waiting behind the door. He'd missed him all week, but today was different. He wasn't in the kitchen like he would normally be if Mum and Dad were at work, but they were in the garden. Jake heard the gate open and the letterbox rattle as a letter was pushed through it. Jake jumped up to the letterbox and grabbed the letter coming through. The postman didn't let go on the other side, so Jake just hung there, holding onto the letter for dear life. He growled, hoping the postman would give up, but not a chance. Jake pushed his back legs against the door, trying to get more purchase on the letter. That did the trick. The postman let go, and Jake fell to the floor. the letter in his mouth. He shook it, spraying bits of paper all over the hall. Jake – 2, objects – 0. After that, Coral always got to the post before Jake. The letter he'd destroyed was a cheque from the gas board. Bruce had to make a lovely call to them asking for a replacement. He got the feeling he wasn't the first with that excuse, or the last, for that matter.

Coral and Bruce were so happy they had found Jake.

He was quirky, full of beans, and he had made their lives complete. They loved his temper and the fact that he would never back down or give up. Jake had at last found his forever home.

8

Hero number 2: Sammy the whippet. Rachelle and Robert Howard had been checking registered whippet breeders for months, and finally, they had found one with the dog of their dreams. He sounded perfect. Sammy was a brindle whippet; brindle is black stripes on a reddish base, very striking. He was a direct descendant of the 2018 Crufts winner and had a fancy kennel-registered name, but Rachelle and Robert decided they would call him Sammy, and they couldn't wait to meet him. They contacted the kennel to arrange a meeting and of course make sure Sammy would be comfortable with them. The kennel was in Edinburgh, so they set off on the 4-and-a-half-hour journey to meet him, and fingers crossed, to bring him home. This journey would be the longest of their lives, so they decided to pass the time and play the number plate game. Now, reader, if you've never played the number plate game, then you've definitely missed out, and next time you are on a long journey, this will pass the time. You take the first two letters of a car number plate and make a first name with the first letter and a surname with the second letter. So, if the number plate is WN53 ODN, then you could pick WAYNE NICHOLS. You keep going around with all the people in the car until you run out of names, then you use the next car's number plate you see. Simple and fun!!!

Rachelle and Robert played this for FOUR hours as well as laughing at other drivers' antics and spotting dogs in the back of cars. "That'll be us on the way back," said Robert, trying to contain his excitement. When the sat nav said two miles to go, the atmosphere in the car changed. Rachelle suddenly couldn't get comfy in her seat and Robert felt sick. "It's going to be amazing, Robert," she said, trying to convince herself as well as Robert.

They pulled up outside the kennels, and they could hear what sounded like 100 dogs all barking at once. "I'm glad they live in the middle of nowhere. I couldn't imagine living next door to that noise, and we love dogs," Rachelle said, covering her ears.

They could see a lady making her way towards them.

"Hello, you must be Rachelle and Robert. Welcome to Carolina Kennels, I'm Nancy. Follow me and I'll introduce you to Sammy. He's looking forward to meeting you," she said, walking so fast that Rachelle and Robert were nearly running to keep up. "I'll show you to a secure outdoor meeting place. There is a bench for you to sit on. Once you're settled, I'll go and get Sammy. You can then spend about 30 minutes to an hour getting to know each other and making sure all three of you are happy."

Nancy showed them to a gated area that had a little bit of grass but was mostly paved. On one side was a bench which had memorial badges on it. On closer inspection, these were all dog names.

"My past winners," Nancy said, closing the gate. "Right, get comfy, and I'll go and get him." Then she was off, racing across the yard.

"Like owner, like dog" Robert said, making Rachelle giggle.

A bit of light relief was needed; they were both extremely nervous. About 10 minutes later, Nancy came across the yard with the most beautiful dog they had ever seen. He seemed to prance, not walk. Rachelle held her breath, and Robert held her hand.

"I'd like you to meet Sammy. Sammy, this is your new mum and dad." Nancy opened the gate and brought Sammy over to them. He sniffed their hands then stood back. He sniffed again and this time his tail started to wag. He nuzzled his head into Robert's hand and then … his tail went berserk; he was certainly happy to meet them.

"I'll leave you three alone. I'll be back in 30 minutes if that's ok."

Rachelle and Robert nodded but didn't speak. They were literally falling in love.

When Nancy finally came back, she said, "You three look happy. Ready to take him home?"

They both nodded as speaking was difficult just at the moment. Crying does that to you, doesn't it?

They followed Nancy into the house and signed the documents and took out their brand-new lead and collar. "This is yours, Sammy. It's not permanent because you are not fully grown yet, but it'll do for now."

"He'll need to be microchipped, so when you book him in for his next set of jabs, ask the vet to insert a chip at the same time."

"We will, thank you, Nancy. I'll send photos of him in his new home and garden," Rachelle said, hugging Nancy again, tears welling up.

"Come on, let's get Sammy home. He's got a lot to explore," Robert said, turning towards her with tears rolling down his face also.

Sammy slept all the way home; that's what puppies do. Rachelle and Robert didn't say a word to each other. They were so happy, they didn't need to speak.

9

Rachelle and Robert took Sammy to the vet's when he was 12 weeks old to have his microchip implant and his jabs so he could finally leave the house. Little did the vet, or his parents, know that all the chips were being monitored by HQ to determine which dogs were intelligent enough to become agents. Laura at HQ had hacked into the company computer which makes the chips and planted a tracking system. You've probably guessed by now that Sammy is one of these super smart dogs.

Now that Sammy had all his jabs, he was finally allowed to go out and go into the park. He didn't know whether he was excited or not. Outside seemed huge, with lots of people, dogs, smells and hazards. He had his mum and dad with him, so he was sure he'd be alright. They clipped on his lead.

"Right, Sammy, time to face the big world. You're going to love it," his mum said, opening the front door. "Let's go." It was only a short walk to the park.

"Wow!" he said, "It's beautiful." There were so many things to see, he was a little overwhelmed. All of a sudden, he saw a little scruffy ginger and white thing coming towards him.

"Hello, hello, hello, hello, hello," said this strange little dog.

"Hello, my name's Coral, and this nutter is Jake," said Jake's mum. "He doesn't like many dogs, so we'll see how they get on."

Unfortunately, Sammy was hiding behind his mum, trying to figure out what this little dog wanted.

"Sammy, he just wants to play, I think."

Sammy peered from around his mum and smelled Jake. Was he friend or foe? He wasn't quite sure. Jake stood looking at Sammy. He didn't quite understand why he didn't want to play. "Come on!!!" he shouted.

"Hello, I'm Sammy and this is my first day out in the park. In fact, it's my first day out ever!!" Sammy said, finally plucking up the courage to talk to Jake.

"Don't worry, you've met me now, so I will show you the ropes. I know everything." (Reader, just so you know, Jake doesn't know everything; he just thinks he does).

You know when you meet someone, and you just know you are going to be friends? That explains Jake and Sammy.

When Sammy was fully grown, HQ sent a carrier pigeon to contact one of their agents with a note to recruit him. So, one day, while Sammy was walking in the park, unusually on his own, an old Labrador suddenly, out of nowhere, said "Psst!" Sammy looked about and saw no one. "Psst!" it came again. "Over here."

Sammy could see a dog hiding in the bushes. "Do you mean me?" Sammy asked.

"Yes, Sammy, I have something very important to talk to you about." The Labrador explained he was part of a secret agency that helps to solve animal-related mysteries that the authorities would never know about or probably care about. He was here to recruit Sammy because his chip had registered that he was super smart.

"I won't come without Jake; he's my best friend," said Sammy.

"But Jake's chip didn't register him as being smart. Not every dog's does," said the Labrador.

"Tough," Sammy said. "No Jake, no me!"

The Labrador told Sammy he would need to speak to

his boss and backed into the bushes again and disappeared. Sammy shook his head; he didn't quite believe that the conversation had actually happened. He couldn't wait to tell Jake they were possibly going to be spies, like James Bond.

A week later, the Labrador was back in the park. Sammy saw him this time.

"HQ have accepted your request. Jake is in as well."

Sammy couldn't believe it. They were both going to spy training!

10

Two weeks later, the postman pushed a letter through the letterbox at Bruce and Coral's house. Jake jumped out of his bed to get to the door before his mum. He was ready to destroy whatever was waiting for him in the letterbox. He was too late. His mum was coming downstairs at the same time and caught the letter as it hit the mat. "Look at this," she said to anyone who was listening, which was only really Jake because Bruce was engrossed in the newspaper, which had the headline:

LONDON ZOO IS BAFFLED. TUNNELS ARE FOUND UNDER THE WHOLE ZOO. WHO OR WHAT COULD HAVE DUG THEM?

Could it be the meerkats?

(Well, readers, we know the truth, don't we?)

"Are you listening?" she said again. This time Jake sat bolt upright looking at her.

"Yes, sorry," his dad said. "We've won a weekend spa break at the Mayflower Park Hotel on the 8th of April. That's three weeks away and it says we can take one dog and another couple and their dog."

"Oh my, I need to ring Rachelle." With that, she was off upstairs ringing Sammy's mum, inviting them to one of the poshest hotels in England. Jake could hear her giggling from upstairs.

"Come on, mate, let's go for a walk. This may take a while," Dad said, clipping his lead onto his collar. He opened the front door, talking under his breath. Jake couldn't make out what he was saying, but he didn't think it was good. Maybe Dad didn't want to go to the spa, not that Jake had any idea what a spa was.

When he got to the park, Sammy was already there. He was wearing his straw hat. Sammy only ever wore his hat when the weather was getting warmer. Spring was definitely in the air.

"Jake," Sammy said, "we're doing our spy training in three weeks, on the 8th of April, so we've got a bit of time to train."

Jake looked puzzled; Sammy became worried. This did not normally end well.

"I can't do the 8th, Sammy, I'm going to a spa break. Mum's so excited. I think you are coming too with your mum and dad."

Sammy rolled his eyes; this was going to be hard work. He explained that the spa was just to get them all to the hotel and that the training camp was next to the hotel. It would mean their mum and dads would be busy getting pampered while they hopefully became spies. The hotel catered for dogs, and it allowed owners to take their pets away with them. What the owners wouldn't be aware of is that this allowed for a period of one day when the dogs did their training in total secrecy.

Jake said, "Oh, I see. Sammy, what's a spa?"

A full day of quizzes, agility, fitness and combat training. Sammy was worried; he knew he'd be alright with the first three lots of training but not the combat. Jake, on the other hand, would be useless at the first three but ace the combat training. Either way, they would try their best. And that's all we can ask!

11

The big weekend finally arrived. Both mums were bursting with excitement; they giggled at nothing for the whole car journey, which took three hours, so you can imagine what the dads thought. All of a sudden, Coral let out a scream which made everyone including the dogs jump.

"What's wrong? Are you hurt?" Bruce said.

"Look at the hotel, it's absolutely gorgeous!!" In such a high-pitched voice that only Jake and Sammy could hear it.

They drove up the enormous wide drive, which was lime tree lined. The hotel was huge and bright white, and it had wings on wings.

"It's like a movie! It'll take us hours to find our room," Rachelle said, gripping Coral's hand.

Bruce pulled into a parking space on the left of the hotel. "We can book in and have a drink in the bar before we go to our rooms." He wasn't really bothered about the spa bit, but he was looking forward to putting his feet up in the bar and watching the footie. They climbed out of the car and sorted the luggage, which was on the roof rack as both dogs had taken up the boot space. Rachelle and Coral couldn't wait to get into the hotel — Bruce and Robert, not so much. They walked up to the doors. Standing there waiting for them was a very finely dressed doorman, and he welcomed them in. Rachelle and Coral giggled; this place was super posh. The lobby was enormous. They could see the reception desk over to the right.

"Hello, welcome to the Mayflower Park Hotel. If you wait here, I'll ask Stephanie, our Dog Spa attendant, to take Jake and Sammy to their room," the beautifully turned-out girl said from behind the huge desk, winking at Jake, which sent him into tail-wag overload.

Jake and Sammy were led away to their beautiful room, which had music playing and big soft blankets on the floor. Jake loved music; his mum always sang and danced with him when she cleaned the house.

There was a door to the outside which led onto a field. "The Labrador said we need to jump over the fence and run towards that big tree," Sammy said, pointing in the direction of the tree. "The training is near there." Sammy was off, jumping the fence and heading towards the tree.

Jake, on the other hand, was too little to jump the fence, so he went for the squeeze under approach. Not as daft as he looked. "Sammy, when do we get our nails done?" Or maybe not.

They arrived at an outbuilding with a field in front with holes dug in it and barbed wire everywhere. Jake looked at Sammy, who had a look of fear in his eyes. "I'll protect you, Sammy. I'd die for you, don't worry." Jake licked Sammy's face to reassure him.

The training dog, a big German Shepherd called Rex, came over to talk to the new recruits. "Right," he said, making all but Jake jump.

"Are you going to paint our nails?" Jake asked.

Rex ignored him. "Gino and Phillip are watching you all."

Jake looked around. "Sammy, where are they? I can't see them," Jake said, looking puzzled.

"You got something to say, Shorty?" Rex shouted, towering over Jake and trying to intimidate him.

Jake didn't flinch but just stood his ground. "Yes, I have something to say. You said Gino and Phillip are watching, but I can't see them, so where are they?"

"There are cameras all over this field. They are watching from HQ and they are particularly watching you. You are only here because of Sammy; one wrong move and you are out!!!" shouted Rex.

"I'm not deaf, so there's no need to shout!" Jake shouted back.

Rex turned and walked away. That was the first time he'd ever been put in his place, and by a little dog, no less.

"Right, everyone, the first task is waiting for you. Everyone to their places. This task is called A, B or C. There are ink pads at the side of the quiz: put your nose in the ink, pick a letter you think is the answer, and press your nose on that letter.

Sammy aced it. Jake, however, got annoyed and ate his — *not a good start*, Sammy thought. Next, agility. Sammy had long legs, so he didn't do so well, whereas Jake was amazing. He was so close to the ground; he whizzed around and beat all the other dogs. Next was fitness. Sammy was built for running and speed, so he was literally like a whippet. He left everyone in his wake. "Eat my dust," he said as he flew by. Jake wasn't built for speed; he was quite muscular and didn't do well at all. Then came combat. Each dog had to go into the outbuilding and "hunt" for the pretend villains. Sammy and Jake stood waiting for their turn. It felt like hours. Sammy started to pace nervously, but Jake just sat and stared at the other dogs coming out of the house after their turns to see if he could tell by their faces if it had gone well or not.

Then, "Sammy," the trainer said, "your turn."

Sammy looked at Jake. "Good luck, mate. I'm here

when you're done." Sammy walked into the building. Jake waited for his friend, (he couldn't tell the time, so he had no idea it was 10 minutes). Suddenly, the door opened, and Sammy walked out, shook his head at Jake, and walked over to the other dogs.

"Jake, it's your turn," said the trainer.

Jake took a deep breath. He was determined he wasn't going to let Sammy down because he knew how much Sammy wanted to be a spy. Jake walked into the building, where in front of him were cardboard cut-outs of villains and members of the public. The object of the task was to eliminate all the villains and none of the public. Jake turned on his terrier mode and destroyed all the villains in no time. He stood looking at all the bits of cardboard lying on the ground, very proud of himself. He walked out of the door, back towards Sammy, and winked. He knew he'd done well for Sammy.

Rex stopped him. "That, Jake, was amazing. You did that in the best time we've ever had. You and Sammy are officially agents, well done. Let's go to the office and make it official."

"Jake, you superstar!" Sammy yelled. They walked into the office to pick up their certificates and go through what would be required of them now they were agents. Jake wasn't listening; he could see a fly buzzing around, so he wanted to catch it and eat it.

Then Rex said, "Can you both raise your right paw?"

Sammy looked to his left to see Jake holding up the wrong paw. "Your right paw, Jake," he said as quietly as possible so Rex didn't hear him.

"I can't raise the other paw, I'll fall over," Jake said, not so quietly.

"No, Jake, put the other one down and then pick up

that one," Sammy said, pushing his nose against Jake's right paw.

Jake put his left paw down, picked up his right paw and fell over. "Told you."

Rex growled. "It doesn't matter, raise any!!!" Rex glared at Jake. "Right, both of you repeat after me: I, say your name, do solemnly swear to honour the agency." Rex looked at Sammy.

"I, Sammy, do solemnly swear to honour the agency."

Rex then looked at Jake.

"I, say your name, do solemnly swear to honour the agency."

Rex just kept going. He didn't have the strength or time to correct Jake. The rest of the pledge was as follows:

I will help, protect and save all animals large or small (even cats).

"Cats," said Jake, "NOOOOOOOOOO."

I will never do anything to dishonour the agency.

I will never endanger myself or anyone else.

This is my pledge; this is my duty.

The training was now over. Sammy and Jake were now officially members of the secret agency. It was now time to get back to the hotel and assume position in the dog spa before anyone missed them.

They ran back across the field and into their room. Jake curled up in a ball and fell asleep instantly. He dreamed about cardboard people and crisps, and every now and again he barked in his sleep. Sammy stared at Jake all night; he was in awe of his friend.

Morning came, and Sammy and Jake were looking forward to seeing their mums and dads. The hotel kitchen had made a full breakfast, dog friendly, of course, for the pair. They were both starving. It had been a busy day yesterday and they had both done each other proud.

After breakfast, Bruce packed up the car and Coral stared at the hotel for one last time. She said, "You know, I don't remember entering a competition to win a weekend spa break here, weird. Oh well."

At that, they all got into the car and drove the long journey home. Sammy finally got some much-needed sleep, and Jake laughed as he snored and kicked out his legs. When Jake's dad pulled up outside his home, Jake said, "Bye, treacle." Sammy allowed it this time; he'd earned it.

"See you tomorrow, my friend. You did good."

12

Sammy and Jake's first assignment didn't take long to happen. It was a dreadful May day and the rain was bucketing down. It hadn't stopped for 16 hours. Sammy got a call from HQ. Some hedgehogs were stuck in the park, it was flooded, and they needed to be rescued. Sammy and Jake raced to the park. They could see about six hedgehogs struggling to find a way through the water; it was far too deep for them to swim.

Sammy ran to the far side of the park trying to find a way through. "There's a way through, Jake, but the hogs are too scared to come through. It's only a small gap."

"I have an idea," said Jake, and ran away.

Sammy couldn't believe he'd gone and left him, and more importantly, the hogs. Five minutes later, he came back with three tins of dog food. He ran over to Sammy. "Open one and start putting it on the ground. I will put the other two on the mound over here — it's higher, so it won't flood."

Sammy couldn't believe Jake had had such an amazing idea. He put the dog food on the ground, and to his complete disbelief, the hogs started to walk through the gap and eat the food. They then followed the food up to the higher ground to safety.

"You are a genius, Jake! How did you know?" Sammy said.

"My mum feeds the hogs in our garden. She calls them Norman and Bert. They have dog food — my dog food," Jake said, pleased with himself.

They checked the hogs were alright and started home. They'd done really well for their first assignment, and they were very proud of themselves.

*

Their second assignment was slightly trickier! The park was home to various different animals and birds. One family that had lived there for over 10 generations was the wood pigeon family. The male and female pigeons had made their nest in a big pine tree, and a new batch of eggs would fill the nest on a more than regular basis. This particular batch hatched and lived without any hiccups until they were four weeks old, but then a huge bird of prey decided these baby birds looked like lunch. He swooped in and knocked one of them clean out of the nest. It bounced down the branches of the pine tree and landed smack on the ground. Jake and Sammy were walking nearby, just by chance, and they ran over.

"Are you alright?" Jake asked the bird.

"I think so," he replied.

"What's your name?" Sammy said.

"Bernard," replied the bird. "How will I get back to my parents? They will be so worried."

Jake knew this wasn't true; wood pigeons don't really care about their babies. He'd seen them pushing the babies out ready for the next batch.

"Don't worry," said Sammy "we'll get you back to your parents."

Jake glared at Sammy. "How will we do that, Sammy? I don't have wings, do you?"

Sammy shrugged — he hadn't a clue how they would do it, but he couldn't leave him, especially with the bird of prey still about. Then Sammy had an idea. "Right, Jake, I'll put Bernard on your back, and you run up the park. Bernard, you flap your wings, and hopefully, you'll lift off and fly back to your nest." Sammy winked at Jake.

Unfortunately, as we've already discovered, Jake wasn't built for speed — he was little and muscular. "Oh well," he said, "here goes."

Sammy lifted Bernard onto his back, and Jake ran across the park. While this was going on, a crowd had formed of other birds and some dogs who were out walking, all clapping and cheering Jake on. Jake got carried away and ran straight into the stream at the end of the park.

Sammy had to hold back his giggles and remember poor Bernard. *Plan B,* Sammy thought.

"Rope!" Jake shouted. "We'll fasten Bernard to it and pull him up."

Sammy ran home. He knew there was rope in his old coal shed. Ten minutes later, he was back.

In the crowd was a big boxer dog. He was the only one strong enough to throw the rope up and over a branch. "Here goes," he said, throwing it as hard as he could. "Bingo!" he said, watching the rope go over the biggest branch on the tree.

"Amazing, well done!" said Sammy, who had held onto the other end, ready to fasten it around Bernard's waist. He called to Bernard, who was extremely nervous.

"I can't do this," he said. "I've never flown before."

Jake pulled Bernard up and up and up. He was so high!

"Keep flapping your wings!" shouted the crowd, which had now doubled. "Jake, the rope!" It was too late. The rope had snapped, and Bernard came tumbling down to the ground.

"Bernard, flap!" Jake shouted, running in circles in the hope of catching Bernard before he hit the ground.

All of a sudden, Bernard flapped his big, beautiful

wings and swooped over the ground, just missing the crowd and Jake. "I'm flying! This is fantastic!" he shouted, flying clear past the tree and soaring into the sky. Then he started to drop.

He dropped straight into his nest, where his mum was waiting. "Where have you been, Bernard? I've been waiting for you. It's time for you to leave home now. Come on, get out."

Bernard sighed, but he was a professional flyer now. You could say he'd had a crash course. "Thank you, Sammy and Jake, I'll never forget you. If I can ever help you, just ask." At that, Bernard flew away to start his own family.

"Well done, Jake," Sammy said as Jake watched Bernard fly away.

"Do you think we'll see him again, Sammy?"

13

Jake and Sammy's secret hideaway, or 'Pack Cave', as they called it, was built while Coral and Bruce had a new kitchen built. Jake used the skips to put the bricks and rubble in. The builders were so confused each day as the skip filled with stuff that they hadn't put in. Sammy dug a tunnel from his cellar, under the road to Jake's house. *Easy access*, he thought. They'd installed discreet cameras at both houses, so they knew when to get home. This had gone on for some time with no near misses, so the system worked. Sammy had also put trigger alarms in their collars, so if anyone parked on the drive of either house, it would sound so they could get home and pretend to be asleep (smart dog).

The Pack Cave had four monitors, each with different information. One had the BBC news on; one had HQ. Jake liked to watch this one — there was an apricot poodle called Laura who he'd had his eye on, but as Sammy had pointed out on several occasions, they would never meet. She was at HQ and that would never change. One had the park, their beloved park, which was a two-minute walk for both. They were very protective of the park; it was their territory, and they would protect it with their lives. The final one had all the cameras from around the country on a loop. Jake never watched this one — it made him dizzy. There were two phones; one straight from HQ and the other from another team in Paris. Neither Sammy nor Jake had ever met either of these other agents, but they'd spoken to them a dozen times.

The Pack Cave was quite cosy. Jake had taken biscuits and other bits from upstairs. (This was before his mum had put child locks on everything to stop Jake from breaking into the cupboards. He could have been smarter about it, but like I said before, he was the muscle.)

Well, reader, I think it may be time to get back to that grass disappearing because the book is called *Where Is All the Grass Going*, after all. Our heroes are on the case — let's see how they are getting on …

"Jake," said Sammy, "let's get to the park. We may learn something from our friends about what's going on."

Jake nodded. He didn't need to be asked twice to go to the park even if it was for work and not real pleasure. Jake followed Sammy through the secret passage that came out near the bowling green.

"Morning, you two," said Boo, a French bulldog who had her eye on Sammy. "Where are you two going in such a hurry?" she asked, sniffing Sammy's face.

"Pub," said Jake. "I want crisps."

Sammy rolled his eyes again.

"Boo!" shouted a voice from across the park.

"I'm needed, bye!" said Boo and ran off.

"Why do you always say pub, Jake? You sound like a crisp addict; can't you think about anything else?!" Sammy said, walking over to the swings.

"I like crisps. Can we go and get some later?" Jake said, his eyes burning into Sammy like a toddler wanting sweets. Sammy had started to walk away by now, and Jake shook his head. He had totally forgotten his train of thought. "Sammy!" he shouted. "What are we doing again?"

Sammy had learned over the time he'd known Jake to always take the lead, not in the dog lead way but to ask the questions so Jake would spring into action when and if needed.

Just then Jake's alarm sounded on his collar. Someone

was walking up the drive. "My walker is here!" Jake shouted.

They both ran through the secret passage at the side of the bowling green. Jake ran up the stairs of the Pack Cave and pushed the panel under the cooker. He jumped into his bed and shut his eyes.

"Hello, Jake, did I wake you up?"

Jake jumped up and down; he loved his walker.

Jake and his walker walked around the park. Jake was so excited that no one would ever guess he'd just been out there. He ran around sniffing every blade of grass and jumping about.

"You are a happy little fella," said his walker. "You do love your park."

When Jake got back to the kitchen, he pushed the panel under the cooker. "Wheeeeeeeeeeee!" he yelled down the helter skelter.

Sammy just tutted. "Right, Jake, we need to find out where the grass went and who took it." Sammy had that look Jake had seen a dozen times, so he knew to keep his head down and get on with the task ahead.

Over a month had passed, and they still hadn't got a lead. No more grass had been stolen, so Jake and Sammy still had no idea what or who had taken it. The case had gone cold, so they put the investigation on hold. In the meantime, a dog toy went missing, so they were busy solving that. This mystery didn't take long to solve — it turned out a cat had taken it just to upset the dog. Most of the local minor cases that came up were relatively simple to solve and kept them both busy from day to day.

*

Somewhere across the country, a hedgehog was out and about one evening hunting for slugs. "What a lovely evening," he said to himself as he shuffled along. Suddenly, he heard a thundering noise, which got louder and louder. "What is that?" He stopped in his tracks as the ground started to shake beneath him. Then the soil started to move up and down like something or someone was pulling at it, and this startled the hedgehog and he started to run. "Arghhhhhhh!" he shouted. He reached the path and looked behind him. The grass had GONE, gone without a trace. All that was left were weeds and moss.

The hedgehog gasped. "I must tell someone what has happened, but what did happen?"

14

Jake woke up and stretched and stretched and stretched and stretched some more.

"Morning Jake. It's FA Cup Final day, matey," said Bruce. "It's a really long walk this morning, so you can curl up on the rug while I watch the match."

Jake liked FA Cup Final day as his dad always shouted at the square thing in the corner of the room. He always got confused about why the people on the square thing didn't shout back. Either way, it made Jake giggle. Coral always baked and then sunbathed, so Jake got to chase bees.

About 2.30 p.m., Jake noticed Dad was getting settled on the settee. He had a big bowl of crisps which, if Jake was lucky, he would share with him. He knew how much Jake liked crisps. Mum was baking gingerbread; Jake loved the smell, but he'd never tasted it.

The square thing was on, and Dad was already shouting. "You are talking absolute nonsense!" he shouted.

"It's not even started yet, so why are you shouting at the commentators?" Coral said from the kitchen.

The whistle sounded. Jake curled up in his bed and dozed off. He dreamed about a world where crisps grew on trees. He couldn't reach the crisps, of course, but they kept dropping off in the wind and floating gently down into his saliva-moist mouth. Coral could hear Jake murmuring in his sleep and wondered what a dog could possibly be dreaming about.

Suddenly, Jake heard a noise, and he opened one eye to see what had made it. His mum had opened the back door.

"Do you want to sunbathe, Jake?" Mum asked.

Jake jumped out of bed and ran outside. *Bees*, he thought.

"Let's get out of earshot of your dad. You'd think he used to be a famous footballer the way he carries on," she said, laughing.

Jake just looked at her and wagged his tail. They both got cosy on the settee on the patio, when they heard shouting.

"Come here, both of you!" Bruce called. "Something strange has happened."

They both walked into the house and watched as the grass disappeared from beneath the players.

"He was just about to take a penalty, and the grass under the ball disappeared," Bruce said. "Now all the grass is being stolen live on TV! What is going on?" Dad looked at Mum, then at Jake. They all sat watching as the entire pitch disappeared right in front of them. The camera went back to the studio where the commentators sat with their mouths open, not knowing what to say.

Jake knew what he had to do, but Mum and Dad were home, so he couldn't go to the Pack Cave; it was too risky. He knew Sammy would be at the park, as his parents didn't like football. Jake jumped up and down in front of the cupboard where his lead was kept.

"Ok, Jake, I'll take you," Bruce said. "Doesn't look like we're going to get any footie now, anyway." Bruce got the lead and then left the house with Jake. "Stop pulling, Jake, we'll get there." But Jake was on a mission.

Sammy was already in the park when Jake got there. "Sammy, Sammy, Sammy, Sammy, Sammy, Sammy!" Jake shouted as he ran towards Sammy.

"Jake, I know, calm down! The alarm has been going

off in my collar since it happened. We can't do anything today. You need to break something in the house they can't do without so that they have to go out to replace it," Sammy said.

They said their goodbyes and went their separate ways. Jake thought about what he could break on his walk home, and he had decided by the time they walked through the door.

"Jake really loves Sammy, you know," Bruce said as he took his coat off.

While they were making dinner, Jake sprang into action.

When his mum and dad finished eating their dinner, they opened the kitchen door to carnage. Jake had pulled all the cables out from behind the square thing, and he'd eaten the end so they couldn't just be pushed back into the connection. Jake sat in the middle of the half-eaten cables and bits of plastic looking so pleased with himself. He knew Sammy would be proud.

"Guess where we're going in the morning, Jake, you naughty boy," his mum said, shaking her finger. "Bed!!!"

Jake put his head down and sat in his bed. He had a really good reason for being so naughty; shame he couldn't tell them.

When morning came, Jake's mum and dad were up early, and they walked Jake to the park. As usual, Jake was then left in the kitchen. He knew where they were going, and he knew they'd be ages. As soon as the front door closed, Jake was down the helter skelter. "Wheeeeeeeee! Morning, treacle," Jake said.

"Morning, Jake. We've got a major problem. While we've been in bed, grass has disappeared all over the country. We've had a report from Herbert the hedgehog that his grass disappeared the night before the FA Cup Final. He was in shock, so only reported it last night. I need to contact HQ. You watch the monitors for the news feed."

Sammy walked over to the phone and called HQ. Jake watched as the people on the news told of their lawns disappearing in the night. Jake counted millions. (He couldn't count, so there were probably a few less than that.)

"Jake," said Sammy, "HQ are baffled. We need to stake out the park overnight. It's a big space of grass, and they think it won't be long before the culprit steals the grass. Jake, what did you do last night to get your mum and dad out of the house?" he asked.

"I destroyed the square thing and the black spaghetti that comes out the back. I'm so proud of myself. Dad's wanted a new one for ages, so I think he secretly thanked me," Jake said, holding his head way up high.

"Jake, sometimes you are a genius," Sammy said, a little jealous because he would have never thought of something that good. Jake did have his advantages sometimes, and that's why Sammy loved his best friend.

15

A few weeks passed, and there were no reports of any grass going missing. Jake and Sammy hoped it had stopped, but little did they know ...

While they slept, something very suspicious was taking place in their beloved park.

Sammy awoke early so he could check the monitors at HQ, and of course, his park. Suddenly, to his horror, he saw it. All the park grass had gone RIGHT UNDER THEIR NOSES! They'd be a laughing stock. Just then, he heard Jake.

"Wheeeeeeeee! Morning, treacle," Jake said, completely unaware of what had been going on in the park. "What?" he asked, looking at Sammy's worried expression.

"Look at the monitors, Jake."

Jake moved towards the monitor showing the park. "Ohhhhh, someone's ploughed the park! Are they planting potatoes to make crisps?"

Sammy worried HQ would now get involved, but they had bigger things on their minds because now not only was grass disappearing in England, it was also disappearing all over the world. It was escalating!

Across the ocean in America, the president awoke early one morning as usual, just as the sun was starting to come up. He could see it streaming through the curtains. He climbed out of bed, slipped on his slippers and dressing gown, and walked across the room to his window. "Let's get that sunshine in," he said to the first lady. He opened his curtains, but he was in for a shock. "What?!" he shouted as his first lady jumped out of bed and made her way to the window next to her husband. To their shock and horror, the whole lawn around the White House was gone!! "What has happened?!" he shouted at the chief of staff.

His dog, Bruno, a big old bloodhound and also a member of the secret agency, knew, however, exactly what had happened; he'd been put in the White House by Gino to watch over the president. He walked down the stairs into the bunker and picked up the phone. It was a direct line to Gino. "Hello, it's the White House. The grass has gone, and I've got nowhere to go to the toilet. Help me, I need to go!" said Bruno, jumping from side to side trying not to pee.

"Go on the soil, Bruno. It's going to be a while before the grass comes back. We've got no idea where it's gone, so we don't know how to get it back."

Bruno put the phone down and walked back upstairs. It was manic in there, people running around talking to their wrists or putting their fingers up to their ears. "People are weird," he said as he walked outside looking for somewhere private to GO.

On the other side of the world, it had happened again. In Paris, France, and in the Luxembourg Garden, the grass had gone overnight, and not a single blade was left. The head gardener fainted at the sight of this bizarre event.

A flock of wood pigeons landed and looked at each other. "I don't know," said one to another.

"Who would know?" said a squirrel hiding in a nearby tree.

All the visitors to the park walked around, clearly baffled. One such visitor had come to the park to walk his dog. His dog, an agent with the French branch, was a British bulldog called Bob whose owners had moved to

Paris for a fancy job (Bob had no idea what they did) about two years ago. This had been the perfect opportunity for Bob to open the Paris branch. He knew he needed to contact Gino and Phillip when he got home; he needed to know as much as they knew, but he didn't know they didn't know anything. As soon as he got home, he made his way to the shed while his mum and dad were a little distracted watching the news. Bob opened the shed door and slipped down the helter skelter. "Wheeeeeeeeeeee!" he yelled. He called Gino, who was desperate for news.

"Right, Bob, what's happened?"

Bob explained very slowly and with as much detail as he could remember. Gino stayed silent; Bob knew he was still there because he could hear him breathing. "So, have you figured out what is happening? Tell me everything," Bob said, panting because he was so excited to hear the explanation.

"Not exactly," Gino said after quite a big pause.

"What does that mean?" Bob said.

"Well, no, we have no idea. Jake and Sammy from the North Branch are working on a plan. I'll keep you posted." Gino put the phone down and turned to Phillip.

"Are Jake and Sammy working on a plan?" Phillip asked, thinking this was news to him if they were.

"No, Phillip, but I didn't want Bob to know we're baffled. This is a lot bigger than some grass in a local park."

It was getting close to the US Open golf tournament, and Gino knew the president was a huge fan, and the whole course was grass, of course. Whatever or whoever was doing this, they would definitely want that grass.

"We've got three weeks, Phillip. If we don't figure

this out before then, we'll have to shut the agency."

16

Bruce was busy cutting his grass. Jake didn't know why — whatever was taking the grass would definitely have a go on this lawn. It was the start of the US Open today. There had been no further grass disappearances since the White House and Luxembourg Garden, so why would they take the grass at the golf?

"Hopefully, they won't take the grass at the golf. Whatever is taking it is full up by now," said Jake's dad.

"You think they're eating it?" said his mum.

"What else? Makes sense to me unless they have a new house and need the grass."

Jake sighed. His dad was so smart; maybe some of it would rub off.

"Right, we're going out for lunch, Jake. Be good," said his dad as they got their coats on.

The kitchen door shut, then Jake heard the front door, then the car doors, then the car reversing off the drive. Jake pushed the panel under the cooker and started down the helter skelter. "Wheeeeeeeee! Morning, treacle."

Sammy sighed. "Right, Jake, we need a plan. I've found a cat across the street who thinks he may have seen something, so we need to interview him. Please don't be a dog. Put your Agency head on. I need you on your A game."

Jake had no idea what 'don't be a dog' or 'A game' meant, but he would try not to let Sammy down.

The first problem was crossing the road; it was a pedestrian crossing, so they had to press the button for the lights to stop the traffic. They walked towards the crossing.

"I have an idea," said Jake. "Get on my back, Sammy.

You are taller than me, so you can reach the button."

Sammy stopped and decided it wasn't worth explaining. He climbed onto Jake's back, pressed the button, then climbed back down. Soon enough, the crossing noise sounded, so they knew they could go; dogs are colour blind, so they can't tell red or green apart. Sammy had tried in the past to explain it was the top running man they needed to look at, but Jake ran off down the street looking for a running man.

As they walked across the road, a little girl in the passenger seat of her mother's car pointed. "Mummy, Mummy, those two dogs have just pressed the button and are walking across the road."

"I've told you to stop making things up, Megan. You need to stop lying," her mother said. At that, Jake looked straight at the little girl and winked.

"Mummy ... doesn't matter."

They crossed the road and walked towards the fence where the cat was sitting.

"Hello," Sammy said.

"Who's this?" asked the cat. He wouldn't give his name so that he couldn't be called as a witness if this crime went to court.

"This is Jake. He's my best friend and he's an agent too. Right, can you explain what you witnessed?"

The cat stretched and pushed all his claws out. "Well," he said, "I saw something weird and quite unexplainable."

At this, Jake got impatient. "Spill it, cat, or I'll spill you," he barked.

Sammy knew this would happen. Jake had no patience at the best of times, but when a cat was involved, no chance. "Jake, go and count red cars," he said.

Remember, dogs can't see colours and Jake couldn't count, so that should keep him busy.

Now Jake had gone, Sammy could get down to business with no interruption. "Right, cat, what did you see?" Sammy said calmly.

The cat sat up. "Well, two nights ago while I was hunting for my dinner, I saw what looked like a large rat coming from under the bushes, but it couldn't have been a rat as it had no tail and was long haired." The cat looked so happy with himself because he knew more than a dog did.

Sammy thanked the cat and went to find Jake, who was happily counting red cars near the crossing. "Did the cat help?" he said when Sammy caught up to him.

"Yes, he did, actually. He saw a rat-type creature with no tail and more fur," Sammy replied.

"Stupid cat, there's no such animal. He's made it up to get attention. That's what cats are like. I've counted hundreds of red cars. Ooh there's another one and another and another," Jake said, very pleased with himself.

"You can stop now, Jake; we're done here. Time to cross the road again and get back to the park." Sammy stood on Jake's back to reach the pedestrian crossing button.

"And another!" Jake shouted up to him.

Sammy realised Jake would now be counting cars all day and made a mental note that the next time he needed him out of the way, he'd have to pick another task. They crossed the road and made their way to the park, where they could see movement at the bowling green.

"Let's see what's going on," Sammy said to Jake.

As they walked, Jake started to hum. He started to get louder, and then his tail started to wag. Then he took two steps forward and four back. Sammy stopped and turned to see Jake dancing! The humming then turned to singing.

My loneliness is killing me (and I)
I must confess I still believe (still believe)
When I'm not with you I lose my mind
Give me a sign
Hit me, baby, one more … "What?"

"What are you doing, Jake?" said Sammy, staring straight at Jake, who was dancing and singing so loudly that it would surely draw the attention of any passersby.

"I love Britney Spears," Jake said as a huge smile came across his face.

"Jake, focus! We've got a job to do. We need to stop the rat with no tail and more fur before things get any worse." Sammy sounded annoyed by the strange singing and dancing. Even for Jake this was weird.

The warden of the bowling green was putting up posters; that's why they'd seen movement. It was the annual bowling tournament hosted by the local pub, The Yellow-Jack Inn. It was the biggest event in the calendar, and teams from across the county would be here.

"Jake, we can't let the grass disappear from the bowling green. That has to be our priority. We must think of a way of catching the animal, if it is an animal, and putting a stop to this." Sammy said, a little breathless. He was starting to get nervous; this had gone on long enough.

THE YELLOW-JACK INN

Annual Crown Green Bowling Tournament

Sunday 20th July from 11am

There will be stalls selling books, cakes, tea, and coffee. The bar will be open for snacks, and we have a special ale for the day called Bowling Blonde. All proceeds will go to the retired bowling club members for their annual day trip to sunny Blackpool.

There will be 1st, 2nd, and 3rd prizes, with trophies for:

best dressed bowler

best dressed partner

best behaved dog

best behaved child

tastiest cake

best stall

Everyone welcome, let's have a great tournament.

Bring umbrellas, wellies, and your own chairs.

17

Gino and Phillip awoke early. They needed to get to their secret HQ. It had been on the news that Central Park had been hit in the night; not a single blade of grass was left. This was getting serious now. They both decided they needed to do something they had never done. They needed to contact Sammy and Jake. It was time to finally meet them. They waited for their mum and dad to go to work, then made their way to their secret location near Regent's Park, where Laura was. Maybe she could think of a way for them to meet their counterparts across the country.

They made their way across the park into the shed where they had met Donald for the first time. This was the perfect place to put the entrance to the secret hideout as no one could see them enter. Phillip pulled the potting table to one side to reveal a hatch and pulled the cord that was fastened to the trap door underneath, where they had installed a slide. Laura had found the slide in a skip outside the park. The groundskeeper had thrown it out when a new one had been bought for the children's play area. The slide led to the underground lair.

This is where the magic happens, thought Gino. "Wheeeeeeeeeee," he shouted as he went down the slide.

"Morning, gentlemen," said Laura as they hit the bottom. "Have you seen the news? Central Park has been attacked in the night. The internet is full of conspiracy theories about what is happening." Laura had clearly been up most of the night. "I've had an idea. You need to meet Sammy and Jake — this needs more than two heads," she said, not even looking up at them, she was so focused on a plan. "Come over here and listen. I don't want to repeat myself."

Gino and Phillip did as they were told. They knew not to argue with her.

"Right," she said. "I am going to send a letter to Mr and Mrs Howard and Mr and Mrs Ward, asking them to enter a competition for the best looking dog. You four are the only ones being entered, so two of you will certainly win. I haven't decided which two yet, but I will. I will pick a hotel which lets dogs stay, organise the photographer and promotion team, and book the rooms."

Gino and Phillip were in awe. Laura was amazing. They couldn't run the agency without her.

She kept going. "You can then meet Jake and Sammy and sort out a plan. The Olympics start on the 26th of July, and it's the middle of May already, so this must be stopped before then. Paris has put a lot of money and time into these Olympics and rebuilding Notre Dame, so we must work fast." She stopped and finally looked at them both. They both nodded in agreement; she was right. They just weren't sure how to stop it as they didn't know what was doing it.

"I've had word from Sammy that a cat they spoke to yesterday (he wouldn't give his name) saw a rat-like creature with no tail and more fur digging around their park a few nights ago. It's a lead, just not sure if it helps."

Gino looked at Phillip. "A rat-like creature? What?!" he said, sitting down.

"I will get the letters sent to your parents and watch the screens for more in the news." Laura turned back to her computer and started typing. Phillip and Gino sat in front of the TVs hoping for inspiration. Laura, on the other hand, was typing like a mad dog!!!

18

"Morning, coffee?" said Robert, who was sitting in the kitchen reading the paper with a coffee in his hand.

"Yes, please. I'll get the rest of the post." Rachelle walked past him and straight to the door, where a very important letter was waiting for her. "Ohhh, this one looks posh." She walked back into the kitchen hoping Robert would acknowledge her, but he didn't, of course. He knew whatever was in the post was about to cost him money. She opened the letter …

Mr and Mrs Howard
Rose Cottage
Bentleyheath
Somewhere in England

Mutt Monthly Magazine
Some Office Building
Somewhere else in England

Dear Mr and Mrs Howard

You recently filled in a questionnaire at your local vets regarding your beautiful dog Sammy. Well, that questionnaire has been forwarded to ourselves to be entered into a competition to win a photoshoot to have your dog featured on the cover of our magazine, Mutt Monthly. They will also, along with you, both stay overnight in the Grand Plaza Hotel in London's Mayfair with all meals and drinks included in the prize. Our magazine features health and well-being information and helpful tips on training and making sure your dog is fulfilled and not bored or lonely. All we need from you is a photo of your dog and a little bit of information about him. For example, is he a rescue dog or have you had him from a puppy? The closing date for entries is the 2nd of June.

We look forward to receiving your photos, and good luck.

Sincerely

Miss F Hawkins
Assistant Editor

"Wow, our dog could be famous!" Rachelle said in a high pitched, extremely excited voice.

Robert sighed. "How much will it cost us?"

"Stick in the mud! Nothing, it's all included in the prize!" she shouted as she walked through the door. "I'm off to see Coral; she'll be excited for us." Little did she know that Coral had the same letter, and she was on her way round to see her friend to tell her the amazing news. They met halfway and decided to walk around the park, see how the bowling competition was going, and see if they could help in any way, while talking about a very different competition.

"If either of us win, then the other should book a room so we can all go together. It wouldn't be the same without us all enjoying it," Coral said.

Rachelle agreed. They would be happy if either of their dogs won, and for the dog and couple for the honour.

They'd been walking for three hours when Coral said, "I'd better get home. Look at the time!"

Rachelle replied, "I'll take some photos of Sammy and send you them so we can decide between us which one is best."

Coral said she would do the same, and they hugged and parted ways. When Coral finally came back, Jake had gone to hide; he knew what this meant. Haircut, bath and brush!!! NO!!!!!!!

"Where's Jake?" she said as she walked through the door. "We've got some posh photos to take."

Bruce didn't even look up; he knew this was going to be expensive.

"Sammy's had a letter too, so whoever wins, the other will go with them for encouragement."

It was going to be expensive, even more so if they didn't win.

"Jake, it's time for a bath. You need to look beautiful for your photos."

Jake was hiding in the bushes. "No chance of finding me here," he said, feeling pleased with himself.

"Oh, Jake, I can see your tail. Come here," she said, picking him up.

He tried to make his body as stiff as possible so she couldn't grab him, but too late, he was having a bath. The guys in the park were going to laugh at him later. Unfortunately, Sammy was having the same treatment back at his home. At least they would both look daft later.

Across the country, Natalie and Mick had also received the same letter. They had two dogs, but one was slightly easier to bathe than the other.

"It's a nice day. I'll hose Phillip down in the garden," Mick said.

Phillip thought *great, I get the short straw, do I?* Gino, on the other hand, fitted in the kitchen sink quite nicely. Neither of them had long hair, unlike Jake, so no haircut, just a bath and Phillip's favourite bit, the blow dry.

It was now time to take photos,

Jake first

Then Sammy

Then Gino

Then Phillip

19

"Morning, Sammy," said his mum. "We're off to work. I'll be home about 1 p.m. to take you to the park. Have a good day!" She had no idea of what Sammy got up to while she was at work — probably best she didn't find out. Sammy heard the door shut and then the car drove away. Time to spring into action! He crawled into the opening under the cooker and slid down the chute.

"Breaking news: The Eurasian Steppe has completely disappeared," said the newsreader on the BBC.

This was huge as this is the largest expanse of grassland in the world, spanning 5000 miles from Hungary to China.

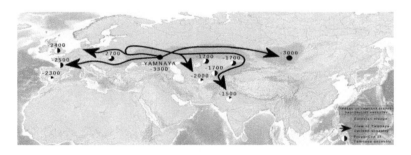

"Wheeeeeeeee! Morning, treacle," said Jake as he went down the slide.

"Jake, we have a serious problem," Sammy said, panicking. "Last night, the Eurasian Steppe was targeted. This is now a major problem. I need to contact HQ and ask Gino and Phillip what to do."

Jake paused and started to sing, *Oooh, sometimes, the truth is harder than the pain inside.*

"What are you doing, Jake? Are you singing?" Sammy said (with maybe a little bit of anger in his voice).

"You said *Erasure* had been attacked, and Mum loves that band."

Sammy didn't have the strength to correct him or explain. He called Gino for advice instead.

"Morning, Sammy. I know, I've seen the news. We've already set a plan in motion. Sit tight, and we'll be in touch very soon." Gino hung up, much to Sammy's dismay.

"Jake, we need to set a trap. We need to catch this rat-like creature with no tail and more fur; that's if the cat was telling the truth."

"Sammy, I can have another go at the cat if that will help."

Sammy did not like the sound of that. He knew that would only end in carnage. "No, Jake, go home and think of a way we can set a trap. See you tomorrow."

At that, they went their separate ways. Jake had never seen Sammy so down. He was going to think really hard of a way to trap the creature and make Sammy proud of him.

When Rachelle and Robert got home from work that night, there was a very posh letter waiting for them on the door mat.

"Oh my!!! Sammy came second in the competition at the Grand Plaza Hotel. It looks like we're off to London for the weekend!" Rachelle shouted, scaring poor Sammy.

"Oh great, you'd better ring Coral. I'm not going to a posh hotel without Bruce. I need support," said Robert, realising this was definitely going to be expensive now Sammy had come second.

"Sammy, you came second. I wonder who won?" she said, reading the letter again.

Sammy was smart; he figured this was what Gino had meant when he said he'd set a plan in motion. This was the only way he could get them together and work out a plan.

"I'm off to see Coral. We've got so much to sort out with outfits, jewellery, which car will we go in!! Oh, this will be great. Well done, Sammy," she said, giving Sammy a massive hug. Then she was out the door and nearly running down the street to Coral's house.

Rachelle was gone for hours. Robert kept looking at his watch. "The longer she is, the more money it'll cost," he said.

Sammy knew the real reason he'd come second, but obviously, he just couldn't tell his dad. The grassland disappearing was major news. All the wildlife and climate experts were really worried, so Sammy knew they had to catch whatever was doing this.

20

The big weekend was here, when all the dogs would finally meet. Sammy was really worried. There had never been a reason to meet before, so this was huge. Jake, on the other hand, had no idea what was going on, and Sammy thought it was probably for the best. Coral was busy packing for the three of them, and the suitcase was open in the front room. Jake kept picking up his toys and putting them in, so every time his mum came downstairs, she found another toy.

"No, Jake, Daisy Moo can't come," she said, taking out the toy and putting it on the kitchen counter so he couldn't reach it.

All three households were so excited, but little did they know the real reason this was happening. Gino and Phillip had to come up with a plan, which they then had to explain to Sammy, but they didn't really want to include Jake. Gino always thought he wasn't clever enough to be in the agency and was here by default.

Coral and Rachelle had decided they would all go in one car as it made more sense. The two dogs were fastened in their cages, the suitcases were stored on the roof rack, and they were off. *Only 30 minutes late; this is a world record*, Robert thought. The Fletchers, on the other hand, were dead on time — you could say with military precision. The two cars left from different parts of the country, destined to meet for a common purpose.

"Shall we put some music on to help the journey go quicker?" said Robert.

"Yes, let's have some greatest hits."

All of a sudden, Jake and Sammy started to bark and howl (well, to their parents that's what it sounded like, but in fact they were both singing).

I just can't get you out of my head
Boy, your love is all I think about
I just can't get you out of my head
Boy, it's more than I dare to think about.

The two dogs were swinging their tails back and forth.

"If I didn't know any better, I'd say those two are dancing and singing," said Coral.

"Don't be daft. Dogs can't hear music," said Bruce, not really believing what he'd just said.

The car behind had a little boy sitting in the back, and as they overtook Rachelle and Robert's car, he glanced at the two dogs. They were swinging their whole back ends from side to side. "Look, Mummy, those dogs are dancing," he said, trying to get his mum's attention.

"If you don't stop making things up, Santa won't come this year," she said, keeping her eyes fixed firmly on the road.

"Sammy, it's been ages since you acted like a dog and not a secret agent. Thank you for singing with me," Jake said, looking at his best friend through the cage bars.

"Sorry, Jake, this case has been really hard on both of us. When it's over, I promise we'll be dogs. Well, until the next case anyway." Sometimes Sammy missed being just a dog, but he knew the good they were doing.

After a couple of comfort stops, mostly for the dogs, and a few hours of driving, our heroes and their parents arrived at the most beautiful hotel they'd ever seen.

"Wow," said Coral, nudging Bruce, who'd fallen asleep about an hour back.

"What?" he said as he woke up.

"We're here," Coral said, a little disgusted. "Come on, let's see where we need to be for the photo shoot."

Robert led the way. Don't forget, he was a very proud father; his best boy had won second place, after all. He secretly wondered which dog had beaten Sammy because in his eyes, no dog was more perfect.

The party of six walked into the hotel.

"Hello, you must be Sammy," a young gentleman said from behind the desk. "I'm Anthony, and I'll be booking you in. I'll show you to the function room where you'll meet the photographer and the event coordinator," he said, looking at his screen while typing what seemed like 100 words a minute. "Right, that's done. I'll take you all to the function room where you'll go through what will happen today, and then when you're done, you'll be shown to your rooms. We've allocated the best rooms in the hotel to you lucky dogs," he said, never taking his eyes off the dogs, who happily wagged their tails in acknowledgement.

"Our other winner is already here, so I'll introduce you all." As he guided them across the hotel, Coral took in the decor. It was all beautiful art deco, which Coral loved. It took her breath away. The walls had white and black asymmetric wallpaper on them. Coral touched it as she went past and soon realised it was material, not paper. There was a huge chandelier hanging from the ceiling.

"Hey, Bruce, can you imagine that in our front room?" Robert laughed.

"It would probably bring the ceiling down." Bruce joined in the joke.

Coral and Rachelle, on the other hand, didn't laugh; they just glared at their husbands. There was huge chunky black furniture everywhere, which looked so comfy, Coral was in love. Bruce worried that when they got home, he would be redecorating. Anthony led them upstairs, which had an even bigger chandelier hanging from the ceiling in the middle of the stairs. Coral and Rachelle stopped right under it.

"Beautiful, isn't it?" Anthony said rather proudly.

"Who has the awful task of cleaning it?" Bruce asked.

"We have a specialist team that takes it down twice a year and cleans it piece by piece. It takes a whole week," Anthony said, pointing to a black double door. "You are in there. Have fun, and someone will get you at about 4 p.m. to show you to your rooms." At which Anthony left them and started back down the stairs.

Sammy froze; he was stuck to the spot. He knew what, sorry who, was behind the doors.

"Sammy, are you ok?" Rachelle said, stroking his head. "Are you nervous about having your picture taken?"

"Jake, I have to tell you something," Sammy said, but it was too late, the doors opened and there stood the photographer.

"Hello, everyone, come in. We've been waiting for you. I'm Boris, and you must be Sammy. Well, Gino is already here. We've done a few shots of him. He's very photogenic."

"Gino?" said Jake. "Gino as in our boss? Is that what you wanted to tell me, Sammy?" Jake looked across the room, and yes, there were Gino and Phillip.

"This will be interesting," Sammy said, following his mum into the room.

"Right, I'll introduce you all. This is Natalie and Mick with Gino and Phillip. Gino was our first prize winner. This is Rachelle and Robert with Sammy, and Coral and Bruce with Jake. Jake's here for moral support, aren't you mate?" Boris looked down at the little terrier and winked. Gino, on the other hand, growled.

Oh dear, Sammy thought. "Keep out of Gino's way, Jake. Don't let him spoil our parents' day."

Jake agreed. This was Sammy's, and of course, his parents' day. He knew Gino's thoughts about him being in the agency, so avoidance was the best course of action on this occasion.

"If you would like to sit over there, Coral and Bruce. You are here for your friends, but unfortunately, Jake didn't win." Boris pointed to a big black settee.

"Looks really comfy," said Bruce.

"Too comfy, don't fall asleep!" Coral said, knowing all too well he would.

The photographer told Sammy and Gino where to stand. Sammy thought Gino would start to tell him the plan for tackling the grass issue, but he said nothing. Gino was in the zone. He was loving all the attention, and he didn't want anything to get in the way of the fact that he'd won, even though this was all fake and Laura had rigged it all. There was plenty of time for shop talk later. He wasn't happy Jake was here, but he'd promised Phillip he wouldn't cause a fight for his parents' sakes. It was their day too.

At 4 p.m. exactly, the doors opened and there stood a finely dressed man.

"Hello, everyone, I'm Dennis and I'm here to show you to your rooms. Your luggage has already been taken up, so please follow me. You are all on the same floor."

"It was lovely to meet you all. Thank you for being so good," Boris said, collecting his cameras together. "I will let you know when the article is going to be in the magazine so you can all take a look at it." At which he disappeared through another door across the room.

The now party of 10 followed Dennis. Coral was still amazed how beautiful the hotel was, and she kept stopping and gasping every few steps. "Coral, come on," Bruce said, getting very frustrated with her.

"Mr and Mrs Fletcher, Gino and Phillip, this is your room, 536. Mr and Mrs Ward, Jake, this is your room, 537. Mr and Mrs Howard, Sammy, this is your room, 538, and this room adjoins with 537, so you can still play with your friend Sammy.

"I'll leave you all to settle for dinner at 7 p.m. We have set aside a private room for you all in our Christie suite, named after the famous author, of course, just at the end of this corridor," Dennis said, leaving the guests to freshen up.

"This is so posh, Bruce," said Coral. "Oh, I love that, and that, and that."

Bruce was even more worried; the hotel would be sorry if he ended up redecorating when they got home.

"Hi guys," Rachelle said, coming through the adjoining door. I thought I'd take Sammy and Jake for a walk before I get a shower and go for dinner."

"Fabulous, I'll come with you," said Coral. She wanted to explore some more. "I saw gardens before we came upstairs. Hopefully, the dogs are allowed in them. We'll ask at the reception." At that, she grabbed Sammy's lead, and they were off, exploring!!! Sorry, walking the dogs.

With their wives gone, the guys could now sleep. It had been a big day already, so off they went their separate ways.

"See you in an hour, Robert." Robert acknowledged them with a wave and shut the adjoining door behind him.

When Coral and Rachelle reached reception, Anthony was there.

"Hello, ladies, is everything acceptable with your rooms?"

"Oh yes, we just wondered if there was somewhere we could walk our dogs. They both need to stretch their legs, as do we," Coral said, looking down at Jake, who was biting Sammy's legs, to which Sammy kept picking them up and hitting Jake on the head. This only made Jake more determined to get his legs. *Oh, the fun dogs can have is endless*, she thought, looking back at Anthony, who was telling Rachelle the best place to walk the dogs.

"You can take them off the lead and they can have a proper run around," he said.

"I hope you got all that as I wasn't listening at all — I was watching these two nutters," Coral said, giggling.

They walked outside into an amazing garden. It was immaculate. "Right, you two go and play". They unclipped the leads and watched as the pair ran in different directions.

Jake stopped and saw his friend had gone a different way, so changed direction and followed Sammy. Coral and Rachelle walked behind at a slower pace, watching the dogs with one eye to make sure they did not dig; this wasn't their beloved park, after all.

Natalie and Mick, on the other hand, had walked Gino and Phillip around the other side of the hotel because Gino had growled at Jake, so they thought it best.

"Dinner might be fun if Gino can't get on with Jake," Mick said.

"He might hopefully get over it," said Natalie, more hoping than anything else because neither of them fancied eating in their room.

It was 6 p.m. when the dogs and parents got back to their rooms. They all saw one another in the halls. "See you in an hour," said Natalie as she unlocked her door.

Thankfully, the guys were awake and starting to get ready, so Rachelle and Coral did the same. The two dogs curled up together and fell asleep. They both knew that dinner was going to be eventful. Gino and Phillip would now tell them the plan, a plan to hopefully stop more grass disappearing.

When Coral, Bruce, Rachelle and Robert entered the dining room, Natalie and Mick were already there with Gino and Phillip. Sammy swallowed hard. This wasn't going to be an easy night. The parents said hello to each other and sat around the table and started to look at the menus. The dogs, on the other hand, were not getting along as easily. Gino growled again at Jake, and Natalie asked him to settle down and not spoil the evening.

"Right, we need to plan, gentlemen." Gino decided to break the ice. "What have you learned about the rat with no tail and more fur? Has anyone other than the cat got a better view of it?" Gino was trying to ignore the fact that Jake was chasing a spider around the dining room. "Jake," he growled, making Jake jump.

"Jake has his own way of dealing with things, Gino, it doesn't mean he's not bothered," Sammy said, standing up for his best friend.

Gino got back to business. "You need to set a trap to catch the culprit, and fast. The Olympics can't be ruined. Paris has rebuilt Notre Dame as a beacon of hope, and these games are so important."

The parents looked down to see all the dogs sitting together. "Look, they are all getting on," said Rachelle.

"We need to think. How can we stop even more grass

from disappearing?" Gino said.

All four dogs started to pace in different directions around the dining room. "Think, think, think," said Phillip, pacing left to right, passing Sammy coming the other way. "What to do, what to do," said Gino, passing Jake, who had found a beetle on the carpet, so he was now following that.

All of a sudden, Jake stopped and looked at Sammy, who was across the room. "Sammy, when we have unwanted guests in the garden, my dad sets a humane trap. He catches whatever it is and then releases it somewhere away from houses." Jake hesitated.

"Go on," said Gino.

"Well, we could set a trap near the bowling green. The grass is the best around as the club has been feeding it especially for the tournament. We could catch the rat-like creature with no tail and more fur and interrogate it to find out why it's here, then maybe try to help it."

Sammy smiled; there was no way Gino would think Jake was not worth having in the agency now.

"Sammy, when you and Jake get back home, that is what you will do. I want hourly reports," Gino said, staring at Jake. So, it was decided Jake's plan would be set in motion. Well done, Jake.

21

When Jake and Sammy got back from their weekend away with Gino and Phillip, they were determined to find out what was doing this. Jake had other questions. "Sammy," he said one afternoon when they were enjoying their park, "what's the o-lim-picks?" he asked, looking extremely puzzled.

"Oh, Jake, have you been thinking about that all this time? You are a daft dog. Don't worry, you just need to focus on the bowling tournament. That's our priority, not the Olympics." Sammy had a plan: they would set a trap tonight. The creature wouldn't be able to resist the grass. It was perfect. "Come on, Jake, we'll set it partially buried so whatever it is doesn't see it." Sammy was on a mission. He couldn't let anything ruin the tournament — it was the village's biggest event. Sammy was ahead of Jake when suddenly, he stopped. "Not again."

Oh, oh, oh, go totally crazy, forget I'm a lady
Men's shirts, short skirts
Oh, oh, oh, really go wild, yeah, doin' it in style
Oh, oh, oh, get in the action, feel the attraction
Colour my hair, do I what I dare
Oh, oh, oh, I wanna be free, yeah, to feel the way I feel
Man, I feel like a woman (hey!)

Jake was swinging his tail from side to side and spinning around on the bowling green.

"Jake, a time and a place, and this is neither the time nor the place." Sammy stared at Jake.

"Sorry, Sammy, sometimes the music just takes me." Jake pulled himself together. He felt a bit dizzy from spinning, but he had work to do.

"Right, Jake, I need you to dig a little hole just here so

we can bury this trap," said Sammy, pushing his nose to the ground to show Jake where to dig.

Jake, of course, being the muscle and an amazing digger, started to dig.

"Right, stop, Jake, that's perfect. Well done," Sammy said, winking at Jake, at which Jake wagged his tail so much he fell over onto his side. He rolled around on the grass, then got to his feet and shook himself off, feeling very proud.

"I've set an alert so if anything triggers this in the night, we'll know. Come on, Jake, let's run around the park and be dogs now our work is done."

Jake didn't need to be asked twice. Unfortunately, he'd never been able to keep up with Sammy as he was built for speed. Jake's legs were too little, but he loved trying, and Sammy was his best friend, after all. After 20 minutes Sammy said, "Right, Jake, let's get back home and cross our paws we catch something."

Jake looked puzzled. "Sammy, if I cross my paws, I won't be able to walk home. I'd fall over."

"Ok, do it when you get home, then, instead." Sammy had learnt to just let Jake be Jake sometimes.

They walked to the entrance of the Pack Cave, climbed in one by one, said their goodbyes, or in Jake's case, "Morning, treacle," and went home.

When Jake got home, he sat in the kitchen and crossed his paws. *How long do I have to do this for?* he thought to himself, but he fell asleep as soon as he crawled into his bed. His paws uncrossed as he dreamed of beating Sammy in a running game.

*

That night, Sammy didn't sleep; he just listened for the alert to trigger. He still had no idea what was taking the grass, but it needed to stop. Just then, *BEEP!!!* The alert sounded. Had they caught something? Was it the right thing? Now there was no chance of him sleeping. He was too excited. "We've caught it, or have we caught something that has nothing to do with all this?" Sammy stared at the kitchen clock, wishing it would move faster. He stared at it so much, he was convinced it was going backwards.

Eventually, he heard his mum and dad's alarm clock. "It's morning," he said, breathing a sigh of relief. "Wait till I tell Jake."

His parents seemed to take forever to get ready for work. *Typical,* he thought. When they finally left the house and he heard them drive away, he knew Jake would already be waiting in the Pack Cave. They could finally see what was taking the grass. He slid down the slide to the sight of Jake chasing spiders along the floor. "Jake, we've caught something in the trap, come on!" he said, not even saying good morning.

Jake watched as Sammy climbed through the opening into the park. "Morning, treacle," he said softly just to get it out of his system.

"Come on!" Sammy said, running towards the bowling green at about 200 mph, or so Jake thought. He ran after him, trying not to get distracted by all the butterflies which were busy collecting nectar. *Must focus* he said to himself. When he finally caught up with Sammy, he saw him looking into the hole trying to see what they had caught.

Suddenly, a voice came from behind them. "I hear you've been looking for us."

Sammy looked at Jake, and remember, readers, Jake's the muscle, so Sammy knew he would have to see what this was first. Jake turned around slowly, a little hesitant about what or who was talking to them.

"Jake, what is it?" Sammy asked, taking a deep breath.

"Sammy, there are hundreds of them. They are small furry creatures with no tail, like the cat said."

"My name's Brian," said the furry creature. "I think you caught my daughter Sandra last night, and I want her back.".

Sammy took a deep breath and started to turn around. Before him stood four (not hundreds, but Jake can't count) ... guinea pigs!!!!

"Hello," said Sammy tentatively. "Why are you stealing our grass?" he nervously asked, taking a deep breath and almost dreading the answer.

"Well," said Brian ...

Time for a flashback, reader. You'd better get something to eat and drink before you go any further because this is a big chapter.

22

A far, far time ago

A long, long place away

On the planet *Cavia Porcellus* lived around 100 families of guinea pigs; no one knew how or where they came from, but they lived there very happily, building homes, businesses, schools and supermarkets. The planet was beautiful, with expanses of grass nestled between each house and with plants and trees everywhere. The guinea pig families knew the value of open spaces and of not filling the whole planet with buildings. One of these families was Brian, his wife, Margot, and their daughter, Sandra. Brian was the manager of the bank. He had six members of staff who thought he was a firm but fair boss. Margot was the cleaner at the bank. She loved her job, and she took pride in it so much that the bank had won awards for not only customer satisfaction but also cleanliness. Sandra worked in the local supermarket, with the most important job. She labelled the food so the customers knew how much it cost— without her there would be chaos!

Everyone was happy until the families became 150 and then 200, and the food started to be very stretched. The councilman decided to hold a meeting and invite all the head guinea pigs to discuss a plan. Don't worry, reader; Brian, of course, being the bank manager, was invited. The meeting was held one evening, but Margot stayed at home. She had organised for a hoover salesman to pop over as they needed a new hoover, or that's what she told Brian. Brian told her to sort it. He was no good at this kind of home stuff. The meeting room was full, everyone talking at once, trying to come up with ideas, which were not really helping as the councilman couldn't hear any of them.

"Order!!!!! Order!!!!" he shouted, and everyone sat down and stopped talking. "Right, if you have any ideas, put your paws up, and I will ask you one at a time, nice and calm."

The paws shot up and he could see 20 or more little paws waving at him. "Right, you," he said, pointing about three rows back.

"I think we need to venture off this planet and find food elsewhere." The owner of the paw sat down, feeling very pleased with himself.

"So, you are saying we need to build a spaceship so a team can leave here and find food?" said the councilman. "Do you all think this is a good idea?" he said, looking around the meeting hall.

The other guinea pigs nodded; none of them really had a better plan or even a different plan. They were happy to go along with anything.

"Does anyone want to captain the ship and lead the crew? Brian?"

Brian stood up. "Sorry, Councilman, I have to stay here with Margot and Sandra, and of course, run the bank."

The councilman looked disappointed because he knew Brian was perfect for the job. "Well, I'll leave it with you. You can pick your own team," he said, hoping Brian would change his mind.

The councilman then addressed the engineers, the guinea pigs who built the bridges, buildings, cars, buses, etc. and now a spaceship! "I need blueprints, and quickly. We need food. I think we can ration for maybe two/three months, but it'll be a stretch."

The engineers started to talk amongst themselves, giving idea after idea.

"Go and start drawing. It needs to be big enough for five guinea pigs at least, not too cramped, and have a cooling system to keep the food fresh for the journey home."

Brian sat listening to all the conversations around him. Everyone had ideas, and some were way out there, he thought as he giggled to himself. He decided that it was time to go. Margot wouldn't believe the plan was to build a spaceship to find food on another planet. He walked out of the meeting room and started down the hill to home. On the way, he bumped into Sandra, who'd been ice skating with her friends, something she did every Tuesday.

"Hi, Mum," she said as she walked into the front room.

"Margot?" Brian went upstairs to find her.

"She won't believe we are going to build a spaceship," Sandra said, walking into the kitchen. "Dad," she said, passing him a note as he came downstairs.

Brian started to read it ...

Dear Brian and Sandra,

I'm sorry, I've left you. I've fallen for the hoover salesman. He's offered me a better life travelling to different towns selling hoovers, seeing the sights and the bright lights. I wish you both all the best, but I'm sorry, you're boring.

Brian was in shock. Sandra cried and cried. Brian tried to comfort her, but it was no use, her mum was gone, and it seemed she wasn't coming back.

Brian helped Sandra to bed.

"Dad," she said, "there's nothing stopping us now

from going on the spaceship when it's built. I think we should tell the councilman we'll go, you in charge and me as one of the five."

"You are upset and not thinking straight. You are in shock, and I don't think you should make such a big decision tonight. Let's talk about it in the morning." Brian said goodnight to Sandra and told her to not worry about the spaceship and to try to get some sleep. *Good advice*, he thought, as he climbed into bed himself.

Brian lay awake all night, and every now and again he could hear Sandra crying. He checked on her, and she was crying in her sleep. *Poor Sandra,* he thought, closing her bedroom door and climbing back into bed. Maybe Sandra was right. They should go on the spaceship and save the planet and the other guinea pigs. Maybe this had happened for a reason.

When Brian's alarm clock sounded, he'd not really slept, so he called the branch and let them know he was taking a personal day. He needed to stay with Sandra. "Sandra, are you up?" he asked as he passed her bedroom.

"Dad, I'm in the kitchen. I'm going to see the councilman today and let him know we're going to be two of the five. This is our calling. Mum leaving was fate, and we are supposed to help save this planet," she said defiantly.

"You are right, Sandra, and I am going to lead you and the others," Brian said, kissing her on her nose. "We'll go together."

It was raining outside, so they grabbed their coats and umbrellas and started the 10-minute walk to the councilman's office. As they walked, they saw one of the bank clerks.

"Morning, Brian," he said.

"Morning, Douglas. I'm taking a personal day today; Sandra is under the weather." Brian said, hoping Douglas didn't ask any questions.

"It is not only Sandra who is under the weather; the weather is under the weather also!" Douglas walked away giggling to himself.

"Come on, Sandra, before we see anyone else," Brian said, walking a little faster.

They arrived at the councilman's office, where Susan, his secretary, greeted them. She knew exactly why they were here.

"He'll be so excited to see you both," she said, shuffling paperwork about on her desk. She picked up the phone and called the councilman. She didn't have time to put the phone down before the door between their offices flew open.

"Brian, Sandra, come in, I'm so happy to see you both, are you both well, you look well. Do you want something to drink? Susan, drinks. What can Susan get you?" He didn't take a breath. Like Susan, he knew exactly why they were there.

"Mr Councilman," Brian said, trying to calm the councilman down before he passed out. "Sandra and I have decided to accept your kind offer and find another planet with food and bring it back to save our species." Brian stopped and waited as the councilman screamed and hugged them both. They were the right guinea pigs for the job.

"Thank you both! What changed your mind, Brian?"

Brian looked at Sandra, who burst into tears. He held his daughter's paw. "Margot left us last night for the hoover salesman. Don't ask any questions. That's all I have to say and will ever say. You can see my daughter is very upset. Let's focus on the job in paw and not upset her any further."

The councilman agreed. He didn't need to know anymore; it wasn't his business. He was just happy they'd decided to help him.

"I'll leave you to it, Mr Councilman. You've got a lot to organise. When you've made the final decisions, you know where we are." Brian hugged his daughter, took her paw and left the office, guiding her through the doors onto the street. Thankfully, it had stopped raining. "Sandra, I love you, and Mum leaving hasn't changed that. I can't think of anyone else I'd want to do this ridiculous journey with."

Sandra took a deep breath. "Dad, together we'll do this, we won't fail, and I love you too." Sandra squeezed her dad's paw. "Ridiculous journey!! We must be mad." They both laughed as it started to sink in what they had just agreed to. They walked home a bit slower this time, chatting about space and being the first guinea pigs to encounter new worlds. What was out there?

The next few weeks were extremely busy. The engineers were working on the blueprints for the spaceship, no mean feat to say they're used to designing bridges, houses and offices. When they finally had a design (more importantly, something they could actually build) drafted, they called the councilman, and he dropped everything and ran over to their office. "I'm here," he said, very out of breath, nearly pulling the door off its hinges as he barged through it.

"I'll give you a minute," said one of the engineers as he passed him a glass of water.

"I'll fix the door while you collect yourself," said

another.

The councilman could see the blueprints on the farthest desk. "I'm fine, let me see the design," he said, knocking the water on the floor and nearly knocking two of the engineers over as he ran across the office.

The engineers looked at each other. "He's keen, isn't he?" one said to his colleague.

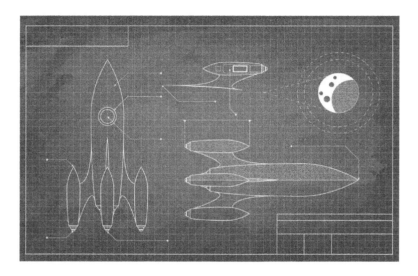

The councilman looked down at the design and he couldn't believe it. "It's beautiful," he said, not even looking up. He was mesmerised. "How long will it take you to build, and what do you need material wise?" he said, still not looking up.

"We need as much metal as possible," said one of the engineers.

"I will ask all the guinea pigs to bring their metal objects here to your yard. Together we should have enough to build this amazing spaceship." He finally looked up at the engineers. "You are all geniuses, well done!"

The councilman raced back to his office. "Susan, call a meeting for the whole town for tomorrow night. We need everyone's help with building the spaceship."

Susan busily composed an email.

Dear Townsfolk,
You are cordially invited to a meeting this coming Friday at 7 p.m. All must attend. This is vitally important. We need your help to build our spaceship to save us.

Regards, Susan
On behalf of your councilman

The email was sent. It was now up to the councilman to rally the troops.

Friday night soon came around, and the whole town gossiped as to the reason for the meeting, but Brian and Sandra kept quiet; it wasn't their secret to share. It was only 6 p.m. when guinea pigs started turning up at the community hall. They were all so excited. The councilman didn't want to start the meeting early: the email said 7 p.m., so 7 p.m. it was. The room was filling up quickly. Brian and Sandra had been told to sit on the stage with the councilman and Susan. Brian had already thought about the rest of the crew; he needed guinea pigs he, and of course, Sandra, could trust. He had not told the councilman yet of his choices, but he was sure he'd made the right decision. Sandra was starting to fidget as she had sat for over an hour waiting for the meeting to start.

Brian held out his paw. "Sandra, it's going to be fine. Once we get the metal, the engineers can start building, and then we can start training. You'll soon be so busy, your mind will be full of other things."

"Right, can I have your attention, fellow guinea pigs!" shouted the councilman, and everyone sat upright ready to listen. "We need your help. Our engineers have designed the perfect spaceship to take us to wherever the grass is, but we need metal and lots of it to build it. I need you all to bring anything you can find made from metal to the supermarket car park by Sunday night. The engineers will start building Monday."

He paused, listening for responses, but nothing — they all just listened. "The more metal, the bigger and better we can build. Let's give our intrepid saviours some room on their journey!"

This time he heard whispers coming from the audience. They were all talking amongst each other, talking about the metal they had at home. Then they all stood up and ran out of the meeting room. It was like a stampede, chairs flying through the air and smashing as they hit the floor. Sandra put her paws over her ears. The noise was deafening.

Brian looked at the councilman and said, "I think that went well."

"We'll see over the weekend," he replied.

Brian and Sandra left the meeting room and started to walk home.

"We will talk to the councilman tomorrow about our choices for the crew, and we need to name the spaceship. We can't keep calling it a spaceship. Maybe the school could have a competition for one of the students to name it." Brian had so many ideas running around his head. At least it was keeping his mind off his wife leaving them both. Sandra, on the other hand, wasn't doing so well. Unfortunately, only time could help Sandra.

When they got home, Brian asked Sandra if she wanted some hot chocolate before bed, but she shook her head, kissed him goodnight and walked upstairs to bed. Please send her some love, reader. She's missing her mum, and I don't think Brian can do this on his own.

Brian sat up a little while longer thinking of his team and his pitch to the councilman tomorrow, and he was a little excited to see how much metal the other guinea pigs would drop off. He was also very worried about Sandra; he hoped that being busy with the journey would help her. Brian fell asleep on the settee, and when Sandra had not heard him come up the stairs, she popped down and covered him up in the night. On the table, he had left some predictions of potential planets where grass could be. The nearest was a planet everyone called the big blue one (Earth, to us). It seemed the best one to start with. It was the nearest, so why not?

The guinea pigs' planet was hidden behind an asteroid field, so all the rockets and spaceships they'd seen going to the grey planet (the Moon, to us) couldn't see them. This was a stroke of luck because as we all know, readers, we humans love guinea pigs, but how would we cope with a planet full of them?!!

Brian awoke to noises in the kitchen. His back was so sore from the settee that he made a mental note, *DON'T FALL ASLEEP ON THE SETTEE!!!*

"Morning, Dad. I made breakfast, and I saw your notes last night. You are right about the big blue planet; it's the nearest, and we can see water, so that must mean grass." Sandra seemed different this morning.

"You ok?" he asked as he kissed her good morning.

"I need to stop feeling sorry for myself. This is bigger than me — it involves our whole species," she said, pouring the coffee while stirring the carrots.

"Are you sure?" Brian asked.

Sandra nodded. "Let's have breakfast and go and see the councilman. We've got a lot to talk about."

They had a lovely breakfast together with carrot, cabbage and cauliflower with coffee and juice. Sandra's nose was shiny, and it had not been shiny since her mum left. Brian had hoped that keeping her busy would help her feel better. Maybe he was right; she definitely looked brighter this morning.

"Let's go," she said, grabbing her dad's coat and helping him on with it. "Have you got all your notes, Dad?"

He patted his briefcase. "Here."

Sandra opened the door, and they were off, striding down the street. These two guinea pigs were on a mission, on a mission to save their planet. Brian was so proud of Sandra; he could never have even thought of doing any of this without her.

They walked into the councilman's office.

"He's not here," said Susan from the floor under her desk.

"You ok?" said Sandra.

"Yes, I've lost my fur brush. It's on the floor somewhere," Susan said, peering from under the desk.

"Found it!" Brian yelled holding it up.

"You are my hero, Brian. I've been down here for 20 minutes. The councilman has gone to see how much metal has been dropped off by the residents at the supermarket," Susan said, a little distracted. She'd been under the desk, so her fur was in even more of a need for a brush.

Brian and Sandra left her to it. Neither of them really

cared whether their fur was brushed or not; the metal for the spaceship was more important.

"Morning, Brian and Sandra. Look how much metal we've had already." The councilman pointed to the biggest pile of junk they'd ever seen. "The engineers have already started to go through it, and they said the spaceship will be very spacious."

Brian couldn't believe his eyes! There were garage roofs, tonnes of pots and pans, bikes, gates, iron railings, tent poles ... he'd never seen so much metal in one place. The engineers were saving the usable bits and melting down the other metal to make the spaceship's body.

"Right, councilman, I've picked my crew, and I've had an idea for how we pick a name for the spaceship." Brian took a deep breath; he had a lot to tell the councilman.

"Go ahead, I'm listening," said the councilman. He respected Brian, so he would go along with anything he had to say. After all, that is why he picked him to be in charge.

"I want Douglas, my right-paw guinea pig at the bank. He's my number cruncher. Sandra will be the grass collector and navigator, Gordon, Sandra's boss, good in a crisis— just remember the January sales stampede — and chief engineer Eric, who is building this spaceship. We need someone who knows the ins and outs i.e. what each blinking light does. I also think we should get the school involved as well. We can have a competition and ask the pups to think of a name for the spaceship. We can pull one out of a pillowcase. The winner of the competition gets a guided tour and a photo next to the spaceship with the name on the side that they picked."

The councilman clapped his paws. "I love it! I'll go

now and get the ball rolling. Miss Furguson, the principal, will love it too." The councilman was halfway down the street by the time he finished his sentence.

Sandra looked at Brian. "Dad, this is going to be the best adventure we'll ever have."

Brian didn't say anything; he was a little nervous if the truth were told. "Come on, Sandra, we need an early night. We've got flight training in the morning with Eric." Brian kissed her on the cheek, and they started their walk home.

In the meantime, the councilman had arrived at Miss Furguson's home and was giving her all the details of the competition.

"I love it!" she yelled when he'd finished. "I will tell all the pups in the morning in assembly."

The councilman thanked her. He knew the task was in very good paws. "Could we have the name by Friday, if possible?" he said.

"Definitely. I will give them until Thursday to put something in the pillowcase, then in Friday's assembly we will draw out the winner."

What a great plan! Brian was a genius, the councilman thought.

On Monday morning, Miss Furguson was so excited to tell the pups about the competition, and she knew they would be too!!

"Morning, pups, hope you all had a lovely weekend. I have a huge surprise for you all. The councilman came to see me yesterday," she started. The pups all gasped when they heard the councilman had been to see their teacher (it was a huge honour, in their eyes, anyway). "He wants us to think of a name for the spaceship, so you can write your idea down on a piece of paper with your name and pop it in this pillowcase. I will have the pillowcase in my office until Thursday. I will pull one out on Friday and that will be the winner!!" She was so excited that a little squeal came out. "Right, you can go to the classroom. I will be there in five minutes; we'll start with drawing this morning."

All the pups stood up and started to walk out of the assembly hall. They were all chatting to each other as they went but not giving away what if any ideas they had about the name of the spaceship.

Meanwhile, Brian and Sandra were at spaceship flying class, along with Douglas, Gordon and Eric.

"This will be a hard week, Sandra," said Brian, looking at Sandra with a kind of panic in his eyes.

"It'll be fine, Dad. You are the smartest guinea pig here," she said, patting his paw and trying to comfort him.

"Right," said Eric. "We've got a lot to learn this week, so listen carefully. I won't repeat myself, so it's completely up to you to take it in. We set off to the big blue planet in two weeks."

Brian took a deep breath, swallowed really hard and got ready for the hardest week of his life.

Right, reader, I won't bore you with the details of flight school. You just need to know they will be ready to go in two weeks. We'll get back to the school and the naming of the spaceship.

The week flew by. Miss Furguson had a pillowcase full of suggestions for the spaceship; it had taken all her strength not to take a sneaky peek.

Friday's assembly was finally here. The pups were so excited that they all giggled and squeaked as they sat down in the hall.

"Morning, pups. I have all of your name ideas here in the pillowcase. I will pull one lucky winner out. The prize is to have your photo taken next to the nameplate on the spaceship."

She took a deep breath, reached into the case and rummaged around. She grabbed one of the pieces of paper and started to pull it out. The pups squeaked with excitement. "I have the winning name in my paw, and the winner is … Georgie, with ZOOM!!!! Well done, Georgie," she said, looking around the hall.

Georgie was sitting to the left of her. He stood up when he heard his name. "That's me!" he said, jumping up and down. All the other pups clapped and cheered.

"ZOOM is a great name, Georgie, well done!" Miss Furguson hugged Georgie. "After class today, I will go and see the councilman and give him the winning name."

True to her word, after school had finished, Miss Furguson went to the councilman's office to tell him the winning name.

"Hello, Miss Furguson," said Susan, "I'll tell him you are here, one minute." Susan got up from her desk and opened the door to the councilman's office.

"Send her in, Susan!" he shouted through the open door. "Hello, Miss Furgurson, have you picked a name?" He couldn't contain his excitement.

"Georgie picked ZOOM," she said, just getting straight to the point as she knew how excited he was.

"Amazing name, well done, little Georgie," he said, jumping up and down just like Georgie had done. "I will go now and tell the engineers so they can start on the nameplate." He ran out of the door leaving Miss Furguson and Susan behind. They both giggled, said their good evenings, and parted.

"Eric, Eric, I have the name of our spaceship!" Everyone at the flight school stared at the councilman, holding their breath in anticipation. "ZOOM!!!" he shouted. Everyone jumped up and down and cheered. They all loved the name; it was perfect.

"I will start on the nameplate now," said Eric, running out of the meeting hall and across the supermarket car park to the other engineers, who were all eager to find out the name.

Brian and Sandra said their goodnights to the rest of the flight crew and started to walk home. "What an amazing name for our spaceship," Brian said, giggling.

"It's perfect," Sandra replied.

They both went straight to bed. It had been a really hard week; their heads were full of technical jargon, and unfortunately, the next week before lift-off wasn't going to be any easier. Brian even thought it would be harder, but he didn't want to worry Sandra.

Neither of them slept very well; their heads were buzzing. Brian was starting to wish he'd never started this, and even more, he regretted getting Sandra involved.

They tried to have a spaceship-free weekend to recharge their batteries and spend some quality time together, but easier said than done. Everyone they saw wished them well and reminded them how long it was to lift-off. "So much for a spaceship-free weekend, Dad," Sandra said, shrugging her shoulders.

They both decided to go home and lock themselves in until Monday, when the training and final tests before take-off would start. Off they went; time to hibernate. Well, for two days, anyway.

Monday was here, and the engineers had five days to double-check all the systems on the spaceship and to make sure the flight crew were ready. It was going to be a busy week; they had a lot to do.

First, the name plate needed to be welded on. Little Georgie was coming Tuesday with his classmates to have his photo taken next to it. Eric was in charge of this important task.

The rest of the engineers ran around checking all the systems, plotting courses and making final checks to make sure the hull was fully intact and fully operational. This journey was so important, it would literally save their race. Brian and Sandra spent their time testing each other, along with Douglas and Gordon, firing question after question until their heads hurt.

Tuesday morning was the big unveiling of the name, and of course, little Georgie having his photo taken next to the spaceship. The councilman was running around making sure every detail was taken care of. It was a big day and he wanted nothing to go wrong. There were only three days left to lift-off, and the guinea pigs were now starting to snap at each other with frustration, stress and nervousness.

"Morning, Georgie. Are you excited to have your photo taken next to the big spaceship?" the councilman asked.

Poor little Georgie couldn't speak. He had his mouth open as he looked up at the huge spaceship and mouthed the word "Wow."

The councilman laughed; he'd been exactly the same when he first saw it too. "Right, Georgie, stand there and hold on to this string. Don't pull it until we tell you to," he said, passing Georgie an enormous piece of string, which had taken Susan hours to fasten together. Her poor paws were sore and rough. The councilman looked over to her and gave her a little wink in recognition of her sacrifice. She smiled back and looked down at her now ruined but once beautiful paws.

"Hello, Georgie, I'm the photographer. Can you stand there and look up at the nameplate? When I tell you, I want you to pull on the string. When the curtain opens, I want to see a huge smile as you see your winning name up there. Are you ok with that?" he said, patting Georgie on the head. Georgie nodded but still couldn't speak. He was a little overwhelmed.

The councilman started the countdown: "5, 4, 3 ,2 … 1. Pull, Georgie!!!" Georgie pulled as hard as he could, and the curtain opened to reveal ZOOM. The photographer's flash went off and everyone cheered. "What an amazing name! Well done, Georgie!"

The guinea pigs all clapped and shouted congratulations. Georgie just stood there looking up at the spaceship with the name he'd picked. He looked at his mum and dad, who were standing in the crowd and smiling.

"Thank you, Georgie, you are a credit to your school, and of course, your mum and dad." The councilman had a tear in his eye; he was very proud of the little pup. "You can go and stand with your parents now."

Georgie let go of the string and walked over to his parents. They held him proudly.

"We have three days before lift-off. These five guinea pigs on my left have a huge journey ahead of them. If we can all wish them well and great success when we see them, that will certainly spur them on. Now help yourself to the buffet that Susan has organised. Thank you for taking the time to congratulate little Georgie." The councilman pointed to the biggest buffet everyone had ever seen.

The five astronauts made their excuses and went back to the hall to cram in as much revision as they could. They only had three days. Eric had been amazing teaching them all this, but none of them had put it into practice yet, so it was all just pretend. Brian was worried that once they left their planet, they'd all panic and forget their training. Three days wasn't really a lot of time, and nerves were starting to creep in.

Sandra, on the other hand, was calm and collected as usual, and she had a way of calming all those around her. She knew no one would let the side down and they would all would do their duty until the bitter end. Brian was so proud of her. He knew he wouldn't be able to do it without her.

For three whole days they locked themselves in the hall, not even leaving to sleep. They just slept on the floor. This was so important.

It was 5 a.m. when Douglas's alarm clock went off. "Morning, everyone. Today's the big day! I'm so glad I'm doing this with you all. I wouldn't want to be anywhere else." Douglas turned to the door so they couldn't see him crying.

The door opened and there stood the councilman and Susan. "Morning, adventurers, are you all ready to save our planet?" *No pressure*, Brian thought.

"Ready as we'll ever be," Sandra said, lifting her head up high.

The guinea pigs got into their spacesuits and made the final checks. Brian couldn't believe his eyes. The whole planet had come to see them off. There was a huge crowd.

"I would like to wish Brian and his crew every

success. We are all so proud of you. Safe journey and remember to come back safely." The Councilman held out his paw. Brian did the same and they exchanged a look.

"Right, crew, places please. Let the countdown commence," Brian said.

The crew climbed aboard the ZOOM and got into their seats. Brian was the last to climb aboard. He closed the door, locked it into place and sat down. He trusted the whole crew. He didn't even need to give orders. He just did his own checks and got ready for lift-off.

"Ready," said Douglas.

"Ready," said Gordon.

"Ready," said Eric.

"Ready. I love you, Dad," said Sandra.

Brian took a deep breath.

"We're ready for take-off, control."

"All good here, Brian."

"Let's commence the countdown on my mark," said the engineer in the control room.

10 ... 9 ... 8 ... 7 ... 6 ...

5 ... 4 ... 3 ... 2 1

LIFT OFF! The rockets all fired, and the spaceship started to move from side to side. The crew got a jolt, then felt a huge surge. None of them could move; they were stuck in their seats.

"WHEEEEEEEEEEE!" shouted Sandra, who seemed to be the only one enjoying this experience. The spaceship had left the ground and was hurtling towards space and the big blue planet.

23

Flashback over, reader …

"You guys know the rest," said Brian, looking at Jake and Sammy, both of whom had their mouths open.

"That's an amazing story, Brian," said Sammy, finally getting a hold of himself. Jake still had his mouth open; it might take him a while to catch up.

"Don't take any more grass, Brian. Come on, Jake." Sammy nudged Jake, who was still a little overwhelmed.

"Crisps!" shouted Jake.

Sammy opened the trap to let Sandra out. "Dad!" she shouted as she ran towards him. "I couldn't get out. These two trapped me," Sandra snapped at Jake and Sammy.

"Don't worry, Sandra, this is Sammy and Jake. They know our story and they are going to help us." Brian hugged Sandra, trying to calm her down and reassure her.

"We're going to help you, and I'm sorry we trapped you. We didn't know who or what you were; we just needed to stop the grass from being taken," Sammy explained, hoping Sandra wasn't going to attack him.

"Where's your spaceship now?" Sammy asked.

"It's hidden in the thick trees on the other side of the park," said Brian, pointing towards the trees.

"Right, stay with your spaceship, and we will come back tomorrow morning and try to come up with a plan," Sammy said.

They parted ways, but Sammy was worried. He had no idea how to help the guinea pigs, and unfortunately, he would have to tell Gino the whole story and why he'd let them go. Gino wasn't going to be happy.

"Jake, we need to keep Brian and the guinea pigs a

secret from Gino and Phillip for the time being. So, if the phone rings in the Pack Cave, leave it for me to answer." Sammy knew Jake couldn't keep a secret; he didn't mean to spill, but he couldn't help it.

"Right," said Jake, "see you tomorrow."

24

The next morning, Jake and Sammy couldn't wait for their parents to go to work, even more so than usual.

"Wheeeeeeeeeeeee!" Jake shouted as he flew down the helter skelter.

"One day you'll fly into the air," Sammy said, as Jake banged into him. "Come on, let's find Brian. I bet he's got a lot of questions, and I have a lot for him. We need to try and find a solution to their problem." Sammy had his secret-agency head on.

Jake, on the other hand, was thinking about what games he could teach the guinea pigs. *I wonder if guinea pigs play games,* he thought, as he followed Sammy through the tunnel.

"Morning, Brian," Sammy called as they walked towards the bushes where they'd left the guinea pigs.

"Morning, gentlemen," said Brian, climbing from beneath the bushes. He was followed by Sandra and the others.

"Right, Brian, I bet you've got a lot of questions for me about Earth …"

Brian stopped him. "Sammy, what is Earth?" he said.

"Well, I was right. You do have a lot of questions. Let's sit over there and start from the beginning." Sammy was in his element; he had someone to teach. He loved teaching, but he'd given up with Jake a long time ago, especially after the clock incident.

"Do you want to play a game, Sandra?" Jake asked.

"What's a game?" Sandra had never played games before.

"It's fun is what games are." Jake was so excited; he loved games. "Gather round and I'll explain how to play."

Sandra, Douglas, Gordon and Eric all gathered round.

"Dad, come and play! There's plenty of time for questions later!" Sandra shouted to her dad. She wanted him to play too. Getting here had been so stressful, and before that her mum had left.

"What are we playing, Jake?" Sammy asked.

"Hide and seek!" Jake squealed with excitement.

Sammy didn't like playing hide and seek with Jake, firstly because he couldn't count, and secondly because he got grumpy when he was found.

"Right, the rules are one of us closes our eyes and counts to 30, the others all find somewhere to hide, then the counter shouts coming ready or not, then the counter has to find everyone who has hidden. The first one to be found then has to count the next time, and so on."

Sammy was impressed — Jake's description of the game was spot on.

"I'll count first, and you all hide!!!" Jake closed his eyes, and everyone got ready to run and hide.

"Here we go," sighed Sammy.

"15, 8, 1, 6, 50, 100, 3, 25, 2, 30, coming ready or not!" Jake opened his eyes and they had all gone. "The hunt is on." Jake ran into the long grass and found Eric first. "Got you," said Jake. It wasn't long before he found the others, all except for Sandra, who had found an amazing hiding place inside a log near the big tree where Bernard had fallen. Maybe it was too good, as Jake was struggling to find her. Jake thought he would slightly cheat and sniff her out; he knew what she smelt like. *I just won't tell anyone how I found her,* he thought to himself. He raised his nose into the air. "Got her!" He ran towards the tree to the big log and looked inside. "Hello,

Sandra."

She yelled, "You found me! I love this game! Can we play again?"

"Yes, it's Eric's turn now to count," Jake said as they walked back to the others.

"Thank you for showing us how to play. I will teach the pups this game when we get back." Sandra was starting to like this planet.

"What's a pup?" asked Jake.

"That's what we call our babies."

Jake liked pup; he'd heard it before but just didn't know where.

The seven of them played all day in between Jake having to go home for the dog walker to take him out. Sometimes Brian and Sammy would hide together so Brian could ask questions about their planet. He had so many questions. He was so glad he'd met Sammy and that he was part of the agency. He knew Sammy could help them solve their problem.

It was 4 p.m. when Sammy said, "Jake, we need to get home before our parents get back from work."

Jake lowered his head — he didn't want to go home, he was having such a good time.

"We'll be back tomorrow, and you can teach Sandra another game."

Jake raised his head again. Tomorrow he would think of an even better game.

"I will show you the Pack Cave tomorrow as well." Sammy had never shown anyone the Pack Cave — he'd never even told anyone about it. He knew he could trust the guinea pigs and he wanted to be completely open with them. It could only help them to trust him and Jake if they knew everything. They said their goodbyes, the guinea pigs went back to their hiding place, and Jake and Sammy went home.

Jake dreamt about playing, and his new friend Sandra. Of course, he'd already decided what to play the next day. Sammy, on the other hand, had a lot more important things to think about. Like how he was going to explain about the agency and at the same time think of a plan to save Brian and his planet. No pressure.

When the next day finally came, Jake watched as his parents went to work, then he pushed the panel under the cooker and slid down the helter skelter, to where Sammy was already waiting for him. "Morning, treacle," Jake shouted. "Come on, let's find Sandra." Jake ran through the tunnel.

"Jake, stop! Sandra's already here. I've brought them into the cave to show them the agency and how it all works."

Jake stopped and turned. "Hello!!! How did you sleep? Are you all alright? Welcome to our Pack Cave." Jake was on overload.

"Slow down, Jake."

Sammy explained about the agency and why Gino, Phillip and Laura had started it. Brian loved it. He was so impressed with the set-up. Douglas, Eric and Gordon were impressed with the technology, and they all sat watching the news on the screens. It was mostly about all the grass that had been stolen from around the whole world, for which Brian apologised.

"We'll sort it, Brian," Sammy said, trying to reassure him.

After about an hour of questions from the male guinea pigs, Sandra wasn't really that impressed; she just wanted to play some more.

Sammy said, "Right, Jake, what game have we got today?"

Jake had been watching a spider climb the cave wall, hoping it would fall so he could get it. "What? Oh, yes," he said, coming back to earth. "We're playing musical statues today."

Sandra looked at the others and said, "Musical what?" Jake giggled.

"It may be best to play in here. We don't want anyone to see us dancing in the park. It would look a bit suspicious," said Sammy.

Jake wasn't listening; he was ready to play the game. "Right, the rules are I will sing a song and you all dance." Sandra looked puzzled. "Move around to the tune of the music as best you can, and when I stop singing, you stop dancing and stand as still as possible until I start singing again. If you don't stand completely still, you are out of the game and you stand over there," Jake said, pointing to the darkest, most uninviting corner of the Pack Cave there was. "Then I start singing again and whoever is left starts dancing again. We carry on until we have a winner!" Jake looked at his new friends' faces, but they looked a little confused.

"Don't worry, you'll soon pick it up. Let's have a try, "Sammy said, standing in the middle of the Pack Cave, ready to start dancing.

"Right, let's start," Jake said.

I got this feeling inside my bones
It goes electric, wavy when I turn it on
All through my city, all through my home
We're flyin' up, no ceiling, when we in our zone
I got that sunshine in my pocket
Got that good soul in my feet

Jake stopped singing and looked around, but unfortunately, Eric was still moving.

"Eric," said Jake, "you're out!!"

Eric hung his head; he wasn't great at these games. Jake started to sing again.

I feel that hot blood in my body when it drops (ooh)
I can't take my eyes up off it, movin' so phenomenally

Jake stopped singing and turned around. Gordon had got carried away and was still dancing. "Sorry, Gordon, you're out!!" Gordon shrugged his shoulders and walked over to where Eric was standing. Now there were two out. Jake started to sing again.

Room on lock, the way we rock it, so don't stop
And under the lights when everything goes
Nowhere to hide when I'm gettin' you close
When we move, well, you already know
So just imagine, just imagine, just imagine
Nothin' I can see but you when you dance, dance, dance
Feel a good, good creepin' up on you
So just dance, dance, dance, come on
All those things I shouldn't do
But you dance, dance, dance
And ain't nobody leavin' soon, so keep dancin'

Unfortunately, Jake got carried away and didn't stop singing this time. Sammy and the guinea pigs didn't even realise — they were having so much fun dancing that they just kept going.

"Jake, we loved that!" shouted Brian. "Thank you. Did you make that song up?" Sammy laughed.

"No, it's a singer called Justin Timberlake. My mum loves him. She listens to music when she cleans, and I know hundreds of songs," Jake said. This time he was right; he did know hundreds of songs and he never stopped singing.

"Sorry, we need to go," said Sammy. "It's Friday, so it's the last working day for our parents. They get two days off now. I'm stopping at Jake's tomorrow night because my mum and dad are going away, so we will think of a solution while we spend the time together. I'm sure we'll think of something. Go back to your hiding place, and we'll come and get you on Monday."

They all said their goodbyes. Sammy showed the guinea pigs how to get out of the Pack Cave and back to the bushes near their spaceship. He still had no idea how to save them or how to get the grass growing back, but at least they had new friends, and they would not steal any more grass. Sammy was worried that if they couldn't help them, they would have to take more grass to take back home.

25

It was Saturday evening when a knock came at the door, and Coral opened it. Rachelle was waiting, ready to drop Sammy off for his sleepover with Jake. "He's had his tea but there's some treats in his bag and his breakfast for the morning," Rachelle said, handing the bag and Sammy over on the doorstep.

Jake usually loved a sleepover as he got to play with his best friend all night. Unfortunately, this night was going to be different. Sammy had a plan to work out — he needed to keep his promise to save the guinea pigs and their grass.

"Sammy, let's play outside. I've got all my toys out so you can pick one," Jake said, walking towards the open patio doors. Sammy followed, but he wasn't in the playing mood. "Do you want Daisy Moo or Mr Bump?" Jake sat on the lawn with what looked like a hundred toys.

"How do you have so many toys, Jake?" Sammy said, looking around at the lawn, which was completely covered.

"Toys!!!" Jake shouted proudly. Jake started throwing his toys up in the air and shaking them. Sammy could see cows, pigs, meerkats and animals he didn't even know flying all over the garden.

"Come on, you two, it's starting to rain. Jake, grab a toy and come inside!" Bruce shouted, picking up a toy. Unfortunately, Jake thought his dad was playing tug of war, so he grabbed the other end of the toy his dad had and started to pull. "No, Jake, I'm not playing you, you daft dog, get off!!!" Bruce was laughing at the same time as he was shouting; he couldn't help it, as he had said many times in the past. ("If I had a penny for every time the little fellow made me laugh, I'd be a millionaire by now.")

Sammy picked up Daisy Moo, who was the biggest toy Jake had, and Jake grabbed the other end, so Sammy dragged him into the house. Bruce shut the patio door and ran around collecting the others. Unfortunately, Jake had thrown some of them into the bushes and trees around the garden, and by the time Bruce had collected them all, it was bucketing down, and he was soaked to the skin. Coral was waiting with a towel. She'd already dried the dogs. Bruce was a little wetter than them, though, and thankfully, this towel was bigger. She had filled the dogs' water bowls and had a couple of biscuits waiting for them. They both took their biscuits and ate them on the kitchen floor, then they both got in the one bed, Sammy's bed (well, it was big enough for two).

"I love you, Jake," Sammy said, curling his long legs around Jake.

"I love you, Sammy." Jake curled up in a ball and started to snore. Well, it had been three seconds, but Sammy couldn't settle. He didn't want to disturb Jake, so he lay awake thinking about the problem they had. However could he save the guinea pigs?

The next morning, poor Sammy had not slept a wink. He'd listened to Jake snoring all night, and nothing had come to him about their problem.

"Morning, treacle," said Jake, stretching, stretching, and just for good measure, stretching again.

Sammy climbed out of bed, not even acknowledging Jake.

Coral came down to let them out into the garden. "Come on, you two. At least it's stopped raining, so you can play out today," she said, walking into the kitchen to open the patio doors.

Jake ran out of the door, waiting for Sammy, who seemed to drag his feet.

"Ok, Sammy?" asked Coral. When Bruce came down the stairs, Coral was standing at the doors watching Sammy. "I think Sammy's poorly, Bruce, look at him."

Bruce stood by her side and watched as Sammy sat on the lawn completely ignoring Jake, who was chasing birds, butterflies, bees, wasps, flies and anything else that came near him. "I'll keep an eye on him. I need to grass seed the lawn; there's a few bald patches," Bruce said while making a coffee.

Bruce grabbed the shed key and made his way up the garden. The rain last night had made the lawn ready for reseeding. His lawn was his pride and joy, and keeping it lush and green was a relentless task. Jake sat with Sammy on the patio watching Bruce first stake the lawn, then rake it, and then he came out of the shed with a huge box.

"Jake, what's ya dad doing?" Sammy asked after watching the weird goings on for about an hour.

"He's reseeding the lawn," Jake said, chasing a bee. "Missed. I'll get the next one," he said, sitting back next to Sammy.

"He's doing what? Reseeding the lawn?" Sammy said, with maybe a little idea coming.

"He gets a big box of grass seed from the garden centre, and he chucks it all over. After it rains, the grass seed grows, and the lawn gets thicker and greener. Dad's obsessed," Jake said, sounding a little bored. He'd seen his dad do this every few months.

"Jake, that's it! We need every dog in the agency to

make contact with all the dogs in their towns and villages. We need to spread grass seed everywhere, but how do we spread it?"

Sammy paced back and forth. Coral was now really worried about him. "Something is definitely wrong with Sammy, look at him," she said to Bruce. Just then there was a knock at the door. "Hi, Rachelle, did you both have a lovely time?" Coral asked, hugging her friends as they entered the house.

"We did, thank you, how's our boy?" Rachelle walked into the kitchen to greet Sammy, who wagged his tail a little bit.

"He's not good, Rachelle. He's been a little down all night. We don't know what's wrong — he's not been sick." Coral stroked Sammy's head, at which Sammy pushed up against her.

"Maybe a walk to the park will do him good," said Robert, grabbing Sammy's lead.

"Well, Jake can't come. He needs his nails cut but he's been playing hard to get, so I'll do them now." Coral opened the kitchen drawer with the dreaded nail clippers in it. Jake knew exactly what was about to happen. He hated having his nails cut, and he bolted upstairs.

"See, off he goes, but you're not getting out of it, Jake!" she shouted upstairs.

"We'll leave you to it, Coral." Robert, Rachelle and Sammy couldn't get out of the door quick enough; they knew this was going to be carnage.

"Come back after your walk and Bruce will do a barbecue for us," Coral just managed to tell her friends as the front door shut. "Right, Jake." Coral climbed the stairs, knowing she had a fight on her hands. Jake was hiding behind the bed, unfortunately not very well as his tail was sticking out, and even worse, it was wagging. "Jake, I can see you, you daft dog. Your wagging tail is a huge giveaway."

Tail, stop wagging, Jake said to himself, but his tail just wagged even more. Jake growled at his tail, and still it wagged. Jake then tried to grab it, spinning around. *Missed,* Jake growled. He spun again, and this time he got it and spun around again and again. All of a sudden, he stopped. He'd spun so much he was now in the middle of the bedroom in full view of his mum, who was laughing so hard she had tears rolling down her face. Jake let go of his tail. The game was over. Time to have those nails cut.

"Jake, I love you. Don't ever change," Coral said, picking him up and turning him over to get at those nails. "They're quite long this time, mate," she said, being careful not to cut them too short.

"Coral, where are you?" Bruce shouted upstairs.

"I'm giving Jake a pedicure," she replied.

"Wow, have you managed to catch him? Well done. Are Rachelle and Robert coming back for a barbecue?"

"Yes, they won't be long!" she shouted back.

"Perfect, I'll get the food ready."

She heard him whistling as he walked back through the house. "Jake, which colour polish would you like? Barbie pink or daring red?" She was only kidding; she always asked him which colour he wanted. Jake replied by licking her face and of course wagging that pesky tail. *Next time I'll hide better*, he thought.

*

"We're back!" Rachelle shouted upstairs. Jake shot downstairs and bounced up at her and then shot outside. He ran round and round in circles. "That dog is mad, Coral."

"He always does that when he's either had a bath or had his nails cut," Coral replied.

"Jake, come here!" Sammy shouted. "Guess who I've just seen in the park?" Sammy asked him. Jake paused, at which Sammy regretted asking because Jake would never guess. "Bernard, the wood pigeon." Sammy stopped him from trying to guess anymore; he didn't have time.

"Bernard, the baby bird who fell out of the nest? Amazing! How is he?" Jake liked Bernard, but neither of them had seen him since they helped him fly; both had hoped he was well.

"He's great. He's fully grown now with a family of his own." Sammy looked really pleased. They had both done very well that day.

"It is a shame he doesn't like grass seed; he could tell his friends to collect the seeds in their beaks and spread it all over the areas that Brian and his friends stole from," Jake said as he climbed the steps to go back into the kitchen.

"What did you just say?" Sammy turned to see Jake's tail disappearing into the house.

Jake had his head in his water bowl, then he lifted his head and water dripped from his beard. "Well, there's thousands, maybe the next big number after thousands, of birds and they could easily spread the grass seed. We could ask Gino to tell all the agents to tell all the dogs in their parks and streets to tell the birds and so on and so ... what? Sammy, why are you looking at me like that?" Jake stopped. He thought Sammy hated his idea.

"Jake, you are a genius! You've done it again! In the morning when our parents go to work, I'll speak to Gino, tell him your idea and get the ok."

When it was time to go home, Rachelle clipped Sammy's lead onto his collar and told him to say goodbye to Jake. Jake always hated saying goodbye to Sammy. Even though, unbeknown to their parents, they would see each other in the morning, it was still hard for Jake.

"See you tomorrow, Jake." Sammy licked Jake's head and off he went.

26

Monday morning came, and it was time to ask Gino for permission to implement their plan. Would he go for it? (Reader, would you mind crossing your fingers just for a few minutes because if he doesn't go for it, I'm all out of options and I don't have another plan.) Sammy would ask Gino alone. He didn't want Jake's temper in the mix.

"Morning, Gino. We now know who has been taking the grass, and more importantly, why. Jake has come up with a plan to get our grass growing again and help the culprits at the same time." Sammy took a deep breath and started to explain about the guinea pigs and the plight on their planet, which explained why they came here and took our grass. He then went on to the grass seed and Jake's dad reseeding the grass to cover the bald bits where Jake had dug to bury his toys. He then went into Bernard and how hopefully he would help with the other birds to spread the grass seed in the areas affected. He took another deep breath and then asked Gino for the ok.

Gino said, "Let me think about it. I'll come back to you in an hour."

Sammy nearly threw up at the thought of waiting a whole hour. "Jake, you can come down now."

"Wheeeeeeeeeee! Morning, treacle," Jake said, hoping Sammy had good news.

"We have to wait an hour while Gino thinks about it." Sammy had anger in his voice, so Jake kept his mouth shut and followed Sammy through the tunnel to their park. Hopefully, they could find something to occupy their time while they waited for Gino! Jake happily ran about chasing leaves, plastic bags and the occasional butterfly.

"Morning, Jake," said Brian, climbing out of the bushes.

"Sammy, Brian's here, and the rest of the guinea pigs," Jake said, getting Sammy's attention by jumping up and down.

"I see, Jake, calm down. We have a plan, Brian. I've told my boss, and he said he needs to think about it, and he will give us an answer in one hour. Stay here, and we'll be back to you as soon as we have an answer."

Sammy and Jake left the guinea pigs and made their way back to the tunnel. Sammy was worried; if it was a no, Jake would think it was because it was his idea, and we all know Gino doesn't like Jake.

"Sammy, are you there?" Gino asked.

"Yes, I am, and Jake is here too," said Sammy, looking behind him to find Jake. Unfortunately, Jake had spotted a spider running along the floor, so his attention wasn't on Gino or Sammy. He needed to catch this spider and show it the door. Sammy sighed. Gino wasn't going to be impressed seeing Jake running about the Pack Cave chasing a spider, but he didn't stop him, either. Gino needed to accept Jake for who he was, not who he wanted him to be.

"Right, I've thought about your plan." Gino paused as Phillip came into view on the screen ...

"It's an amazing plan. Well done, Jake. He's right — there are billions of birds," Phillip said as he watched Jake run past the screen. "We will set the plan in motion here, Paris, and of course, with Bruno at the White House." Phillip stopped as Jake shouted, "Got it, not got it," and ran in the opposite direction. Sammy was trying to hold his giggles in. He loved his friend even if the timing was slightly inappropriate.

"Sammy, you tell Bernard to spread the word. We need to get as many birds involved as we can, and the quicker the better." Gino had a slightly panicked tone to his voice, as time was running out to fix this before the Olympics.

"We'll find Bernard now, tell him the plan and ask him for his help to get the word out. We will tell all our friends in the park to ask the birds in their gardens for their help," Sammy said as Jake ran into the wall.

"Got it this time!!" he shouted. He stood next to Sammy with a big grin on his face and then realised he was being watched by Gino and Phillip. "Morning, treacle," he said. "Are we allowed to put our plan in action?" he asked, looking at Sammy.

"Yes, Jake, well done for thinking of the plan." Gino actually acknowledged Jake, something he'd never done.

This made a tear form in Sammy's eye. His best friend had done good.

They said their goodbyes, and Jake and Sammy ran through the tunnel. They needed to find Bernard first and set the plan in motion, then find their dog friends and spread the word. Then of course, they needed to find Brian and the guinea pigs and tell them their plan to save not only further grass from being stolen, but also how the grass they stole was going to be replaced, and most of all, how to get the grass growing on the guinea pigs' planet.

"Jake, we need to split up. You find Bernard and explain your plan, and I will find our dog friends on the way to finding Brian." Sammy pushed his head against Jake's. "I have complete faith in you; you can do this."

They ran their separate ways, Jake looking for Bernard, Sammy looking for other dogs in the park and other animals along the way to where Brian was hiding.

Jake saw Bernard in the distance. "Bernard!" he shouted, making Bernard jump.

"Hello, Jake, how are you doing? I saw Sammy yesterday; did he tell you?" Bernard was such a polite bird, but unfortunately, Jake didn't have time for polite chit-chat. There was work to be done.

"Right, Bernard, we have a plan to get the grass growing again, but we need your help," Jake said, grabbing Bernard's full attention. Reader, we know the plan, so we don't have to listen to this conversation. Let's get back to Sammy and who he's managed to get on board to help.

Sammy was over on the other side of the park and had managed to speak to about five dogs, who in turn had promised to pass the plan on to not only the birds in their garden, but also other dogs they would see either going to or leaving the park. *The more the merrier,* Sammy thought as he weaved in and out of the bushes looking for Brian. "Brian, Sandra, where are you?" he called out.

"We're here," said Sandra, pushing her little head out of the bushes. "Hello," she said, "Did Gino go for your plan?"

Brian and Sandra's little faces had so much hope in them that Sammy had to tell them straight away. He was worried they would start taking grass again if he didn't. "Yes, he did, he loved Jake's plan. Jake's gone to find Bernard and hopefully start the ball rolling. He needs as many animals to help us as possible." Sammy was so relieved he could give them good news. He sat down on the grass beside them. He needed a minute; it had been a busy day already.

Just then Jake came running over.

"Hello, Jake, did you find Bernard?" Sandra asked.

"I did. He's fully on board, and he's gathering the troops. We should start seeing birds in big numbers dropping seeds in all affected areas within an hour. I think we may even make the news!!!"

Sammy gazed at his friend. "Wow, Jake!"

Jake winked. He had no idea what he had just said — they were Bernard's words, not his, but clearly he'd impressed Sammy and the guinea pigs, so *job done*, he thought. "My dad has got three boxes of grass seed in the shed. I will take one later and give it to you, Brian, to take back to your planet. Sammy will help you with the instructions on the box so you can grow your own seed and keep growing it for generations to come."

Sammy stared at this impostor in front of him. Jake had suddenly become, well, smart. Just then Sammy changed his mind; Jake had seen a butterfly, and he was back to daft Jake chasing it around the park.

"Looks like we're back to normal," said Sammy. "I wouldn't want him any other way. Come on, Jake, we've got to get back home. Your dog walker will be here soon."

"Bye," said Sandra. She'd got a little attached to Jake, maybe too attached. They were not from this planet, and soon they would be going home.

Jake and Sammy climbed through the tunnel and said their goodbyes. "See you tomorrow, Jake." Jake climbed under the cooker and got in his bed ready for his dog walker to collect him. She would never know he'd literally saved one planet from extinction and her own from grass-stealing guinea pigs. No one would ever know.

When Jake and Sammy's parents came home from work some hours later, they had both noticed something strange going on in the skies above them.

"Have you seen all the birds gathering in the park? It's like something out of a movie, really weird," said Rachelle.

"I know, I saw them coming through town too. There's hundreds of them all gathering. What is going on?" Robert said, switching the news on to see if it was just their village or if it was happening elsewhere.

"OH MY GOSH, RACHELLE, LOOK!!!"

BREAKING NEWS!!!! BIRDS ARE DROPPING SEEDS ALL OVER THE WORLD!

"We have no idea why they are doing this, but thank you, birds!!" said an RSPB spokesperson.

BILL ODDIE and DAVID ATTENBOROUGH have no idea either.

It was breaking news on every channel in different countries around the whole world. The president of the USA held a press conference saying they were bringing in the top scientists from around the world to help explain this phenomenon. Sammy watched as his colleague Bruno sat beside his master, looking so proud; he'd also been part of this. Gino had contacted him to spread the word among the birds at the White House, who in turn had told other birds, and soon birds all over America were dropping seeds. Robert couldn't find anything else on the TV. Even his favourite quiz show had been taken off-air because of this very unusual spectacle. Robert and Rachelle watched as huge numbers of birds circled above wasteland where there had once been grass and dropped the seed.

Rachelle's phone rang, which made her jump. It was Coral. Both her and Bruce were watching the news too. Jake sat quietly at the side of his dad. He wanted to shout, "I did that!" but it would only come out as a bark. Nonetheless, he was so proud of himself and his friends. Robert changed the channel again, and this time it was the French president who was holding a press conference. He had been liaising with both the US and the UK — more heads are better than one (his words not mine). The French president was happy the Olympics would not have to be cancelled and that something, or someone, had saved the grass.

Different scientists and animal experts kept appearing on the news programmes, completely baffled as to why this was happening. One animal expert said, "Nature always finds a way."

Jake shouted, "Is that your best quote? Call yourself an expert!"

Bruce patted Jake on the head. "Jake, are you barking because you are cheering the birds on?" *Oh, yes,* Jake thought, *I must keep my opinion to myself.*

Their parents watched into the night. It was so fascinating, they couldn't switch it off.

Bruce suddenly stood up and said, "I need to feed the

birds. There's no food on the bird feeders."

Coral looked completely bewildered. "It's 11 p.m."

Bruce was on a mission, which was great for Jake because it was now his chance to take the grass seed for Brian. "Do you want to go out, Jake?"

Of course, Jake ran around the garden pretending he needed the toilet. While his dad wasn't looking, he sneaked into the shed, took a box of seed and hid it in one of the bushes. While he was hiding, he spotted one of his toys he had left out the last time he was playing, probably the last time Sammy came over. He quickly picked it up and carried it towards the house. *Good job*, he thought to himself.

Coral was waiting. "No, Jake that needs to go into the washer. Look at the state of it!"

Well, he nearly got away with it.

They decided it was now time to go to bed. It had been a weird day for the whole household. Jake knew that soon the time would come when he had to say goodbye to his new friends.

It was funny, a terrier had become good friends with a rodent.

Over the next few days, birds gathered all over the world in huge numbers, dropping seeds. Even pelicans joined in, and we all know how big their beaks are. Soon people were joining in, and the government gave out free grass seed and asked them to spread it anywhere there was patchy grass. Children from schools were taken on day trips to help spread grass seeds, saving the planet and being outdoors at the same time, and the children loved it.

Unfortunately, it soon became very clear that the guinea pigs had to go home. Sammy had explained to Brian how to germinate grass seed for future generations and thus secure the future of the planet. They could come back at any time if they had any further questions or needed help in the future. Sammy and Jake just had one more thing to do before they went. Brian and his friends needed to meet and of course thank Bernard. He had been relentless in getting the word out to as many birds as possible.

"Morning, Brian. We want you to meet Bernard," said Sammy.

"Hello, Bernard." Brian held out a paw.

Bernard responded by holding out a wing. "Brian, it's lovely to meet you. I'm glad we were able to help your planet," Bernard said ever so politely.

"Thank you, Bernard, I can never repay you for your kindness. Just know we will never forget you or Sammy and Jake." Brian knew this would be the last time he would see his new friends. He was very sad to be saying goodbye.

"I need to go; I told my wife I'd bring some food home. That was an hour ago, and she'll be wondering where I've got to," said Bernard, making his apologies.

"See you soon, Bernard." Jake hugged the big bird, who then flew away.

"I like Bernard," Jake said, watching him leave, trying to take his mind off saying goodbye to his new friends.

"Right, we've done all our checks and it's time for us to say goodbye. Just know we will never forget you. Look up to the sky once in a while and say hi." Brian was trying to hold back the tears that were now forming. He knew this was going to be hard, especially on Sandra. She'd grown very fond of Jake.

"Jake, Sammy, I will miss you." Sandra started to cry, and Jake hugged her.

"We will miss you too," Jake said. "Think of us when you play hide and seek," he said, smiling.

"As soon as I get home, I will go to the school and tell the teacher of your games. I'm sure the pups will love them." Sandra turned and climbed into the spaceship. This was too hard to bear. Why did they have to go back?

Eric, Gordon and Douglas were also sorry to go. They had had such an amazing time. They never knew games existed or how to have fun, but they needed to get back. They had a bigger job to do back home.

Brian was the last to climb on board the ZOOM. He turned and waved his little paw, then the door shut. Sammy and Jake heard it lock. They stood back to give the spaceship some room — they weren't sure how much noise or smoke would come out of it.

"I love you, Sandra," Jake said as the rockets fired.

"I know, Jake. She'll forever be in your heart." Sammy kissed Jake's head.

The spaceship took off, flying through the trees and up into the sky. Sammy and Jake watched it for as long as they could, and then it was gone.

27

One morning when Gino and Phillip got to the park, there was a notice fastened to the gates.

Unfortunately, while they had been saving both our planet and the guinea pigs' planet, one of their own had sadly passed away.

MEMORIAL DAY FOR CHARLES (Salvation Army Mascot)
Sunday 7th July from 1 p.m.

The Salvation Army band will be playing on the bandstand in honour of their fallen friend.

Everyone is welcome to come and join Charles's family and friends in saluting this great soldier.

If anyone has any stories they would like to share, please contact Jeff on 07536888690. He will be making love padlocks for the gates.

There will also be stalls, and all proceeds will go to the Salvation Army charity to help retired soldiers and their families. Charles's family look forward to welcoming you on the day.

Joyce and Henry.

Gino looked at Phillip. "Charles was in the army. We all thought he'd made it up," Phillip said. "I feel awful." Gino bowed his head in both embarrassment and in honour of his friend.

Natalie unclipped their leads, thinking they would make a run for it across the park, but today they just didn't feel like it. The grass disappearance was over, and the grass had been saved for the Olympics with three weeks to spare, but the mood in the park had gone from being overjoyed to one of sorrow. Everyone liked Charles, and no one had known he was ill. This was such a shock.

"Morning, guys," said Laura, crawling from beneath the bushes. "Have you heard about Charles?" Gino and Phillip nodded but were too upset to talk.

They walked around the park in silence and started to walk back to their mum, who had been watching them in complete disbelief.

"Morning," said one of the gardeners as he sat beside her on the bench. "There's a weird atmosphere in here today; it's like the dogs are mourning Charles," he said, passing her a custard cream.

"I know, look at my dogs there, not even running around. I've never seen this behaviour. They love coming to the park," she said, pointing to her dogs, whose heads were down and who were walking so slowly, it would literally take all day for them to walk back to her.

"It's going to be a lovely day for the memorial. We are planting yellow and orange marigolds over the next week in squares all over the park. It'll be beautiful. I'll probably see you tomorrow," said the gardener as he finished his cup of coffee and put the lid back on his flask.

"See you tomorrow. I look forward to seeing the flowers." Natalie stood up to greet a very sombre Gino and Phillip coming towards her. She clipped their leads onto their collars and started the longer than normal walk home.

When Mick got home from work, he walked into the kitchen, where his wife was sitting at the table working. "I won't be long, I just need to finish this report," she said, not even looking up from her laptop.

"What's up with the boys? They look like they've lost all their toys," he said, wondering why they'd not greeted him in the usual way, (like they'd not seen him in two weeks, not eight hours).

"They had a shock today when they found out their friend Charles had passed away. I didn't know dogs could get so upset. The whole park seemed to feel it. There's a memorial day on the 7th of July, and the gardeners are planting marigolds in honour of him," she said, still not looking up. "Right, done," she said, finally switching off the laptop and looking at her husband for the first time since he'd come home.

"So, you are saying one of their friends has died and they're mourning?" He couldn't believe it. "Poor dogs," he said, giving them both a hug. "I'm so sorry for your loss. We will go to the memorial to honour your friend." Gino and Phillip responded with a lick on their dad's face.

The rest of the evening was spent in silence, both humans and dogs honouring Charles in their own way, which was maybe a little weird, as Mick had never even met him.

Each morning for the rest of that week, Mick left the house and crossed the road to the park gates, where he could see a hive of activity going on to make the park look amazing for Charles's day. He said good morning to the gardeners, who were just starting work. He stood there in awe. "Well, Charles," he said one morning, "I hope you are ready for the send-off; you were clearly loved." He turned, walked across the road and got into his car to set off to work for the day.

The day of the memorial soon came. Gino and Phillip were up very early; neither of them had slept.

"Morning, boys," Mum said, kissing their heads. "We'll have breakfast and then we'll go over to the park to see if anyone needs any help setting up their stalls."

Gino and Phillip weren't really hungry, but they knew they couldn't go to the park on their own, so they went along with the pretence. Breakfast was finally over; it was now time to go to the park and pay their respects. Natalie and Mick clipped their leads on, and together they made the journey to the park. For the first time ever, this journey wasn't a pleasure, it was an honour.

The Salvation Army band was setting up their instruments on the band stand. There were so many people, it looked like the whole of London had come out to support Charles and his family. Gino could see all the stalls; there were cakes, books, a tombola, tea and coffee. There was even a cake stall for dogs.

"Charles would have loved this," Phillip said, brushing up to Gino, who was a little overwhelmed. He'd never known anyone who had died before.

Natalie and Mick helped to set up the tea and coffee stand that was being run by the lady who had helped Charles's mum and dad adopt him when he was too old to be a mascot anymore.

"Hello," said a voice from behind Natalie. "I'm Joyce and this is my husband, Henry. We're Charles's parents," said this very well-dressed lady Natalie had seen many times but had never spoken to.

"Hello, I'm Natalie, and this is Mick. We're Gino and

Phillip's parents." They shook hands and sat at one of the tables set up for customers of the tea and coffee stall. "We're so sorry for your loss. Gino and Phillip loved Charles," Natalie said.

"Thank you. Looking around, he was very well loved. We're a little overwhelmed at the turnout, and we still have one hour left before we officially start," Joyce said, looking around and wiping the tears from her eyes. "He'd been a mascot for eight years before he unfortunately became too old, and they had to retire him. He was such a good-natured boy."

"Joyce, Sergeant Lewis would like a word," said the organiser.

"Please excuse me," Joyce said and then made her way to the bandstand, where a gentleman met her in full army uniform.

"Gosh," Natalie said to Mick.

It was 1 p.m. and Natalie looked over to the park gates, where there were hundreds of people waiting to come through them.

"Look," said Gino, "our friends are here."

Phillip looked over to see Wolfgang, the triplets and Wayne with their parents. "It would never have been the same if we were not all here."

"Can everyone please come over to the bandstand? Charles's family have a few words to say," came a voice over the microphone. Everyone moved towards the bandstand, all saying hello and how are you as they went.

After a few minutes, Joyce stood in the middle of the bandstand with the microphone. "Hello, everyone. For those who don't know me, I'm Joyce, and over there is my husband, Henry. When Charles became too old to be an army mascot anymore, we adopted him and made his last few years very special, as did he for us. If you were blessed with knowing him, you would know he was beautiful and so loving. He will be missed both in our house and in our hearts. I want to thank you all for coming to celebrate his life and honour him. Please enjoy your day and don't be sad. If you have any stories about him, please come and tell me. I'd love to hear them." Joyce passed the microphone to Sergeant Lewis and the band started to play.

Natalie knew she had to tell Joyce the story of the squirrel and the dogs collecting his nuts. She would probably not believe her, but nevertheless, she would tell the story.

The day was perfect; the sun shone all day. Joyce and Henry loved hearing all the stories everyone had to tell them about their beautiful boy.

*

A few weeks after the memorial day, Joyce and Henry were placing a plaque on the bench Charles always sat near, just over by the rhododendrons. They saw a small pinky-coloured thing moving under the bush. "Hello," said Joyce. "What's your name?" Joyce held out her hand. A very nervous Laura crawled from under the bushes. She was covered in leaves and mud. It had been a while since she'd had a bath or even a brush. Joyce started to feel around Laura's neck for a collar under all that fur. "Your name is Laura. Well, Laura, it looks like you're coming home with us." Joyce picked her up and carried her home.

Laura was not homeless anymore. Charles was still looking out for her.

"Thank you, Charles," Laura whispered.

28

The day of the tournament was finally here. Robert jumped out of bed and threw the bedroom curtains open. "Look, Rachelle, it's gorgeous out there, perfect weather for the tournament," he said, turning to see his wife trying to hide from the bright sunlight beaming into the room. "Grumpy, I'll go and let Sammy out and make some coffee," he said, halfway down the stairs before he'd finished his conversation.

Sammy was waiting for him as he walked into the room, his tail already wagging.

"Good morning, Sammy, are you ready to win best behaved dog today?"

Sammy responded by wagging his tail even more. Robert opened the back door so Sammy could go outside and filled the kettle.

"I think Sammy should wear his straw hat today. It's very sunny," Rachelle said as she walked into the kitchen.

This was going to be a big ... sorry ... huge day for this little village. Everyone would be in their best finery, even the dogs. Two streets away, Coral was brushing Jake.

"It's your year to win best behaved dog, Jake. No chasing the jack or digging on the green," she said, kissing his head. Jake had decided he was going to win, as Sammy had won it last year, so he would do it for his mum and dad. They'd never given up on him, even when he destroyed the post every day.

There was a knock at the door and Jake barked. Sammy barked back through the locked door. "I think your best friend's here, Jake." Jake ran to the door, spinning around only once as he made his way.

When Coral opened the door, both dogs bounded at each other.

"You'd think they'd not seen each other for days," said Rachelle, hugging her friend while trying not to get knocked over by two very excited dogs.

"The dogs are not the only ones who act like they've not seen their friends for days," Robert said, winking at Bruce, who giggled.

"Right, let's go. I've made chocolate brownies, so I need to give them to Maureen before everyone else gets here," Coral said, patting the huge tin she had in her hands.

"I can hold the brownies, Coral," Bruce said, rubbing his stomach.

"Over my dead body!"

The jolly group walked towards the park. Jake kept trying to bite Sammy's legs to which Sammy just lifted them out of harm's way and stepped over the much smaller dog. This made Jake giggle and keep trying.

The gates to the park looked amazing. There were beautiful marigolds and begonias everywhere, and the colours were beautiful.

"Wow," said Rachelle and Coral together.

"Drop the cake off, and we'll see you in the bar. Four pints of bowling blonde coming up," said Robert, pushing past the girls.

Coral, Rachelle and the dogs went straight to the cake stall. "Oh, Maureen, it looks absolutely gorgeous. Here's the brownies I promised," said Coral, passing the tin to Maureen, who opened it just enough to smell the goodies inside. "Coral, they smell amazing, thank you."

Maureen Higginbottom's cake stall was always full to

the brim with the best and most fattening cakes you'd ever seen; no one needed the buffet that was laid on after the tournament. It was a real treat.

Coral and Rachelle sat on the chairs Robert and Bruce had placed on the left-hand side of the green, just slightly in the shade for the dogs.

Kenneth Trilby was the club secretary; he was the one who would pick the category winners and give out the trophies.

"Hello, Kenneth," said Coral.

"Hello, ladies and gents." He was talking to Jake and Sammy, as Robert and Bruce had not come back yet from the bar. "Looking good, Sammy, in your straw hat." Kenneth held his own hat and nodded towards Sammy, who responded with a bark.

Kenneth made his way around the edge of the green saying hello to everyone. He was very fond of his club, and his role particularly.

"There you go," said Bruce, handing a pint to Coral.

"That's your first?" said Rachelle, knowing it wasn't.

"I wasn't sure if I liked it, so it took two for me to decide," he said, kissing her on the cheek and sitting down.

"Can I have the players on the green, please?" said Kenneth over the microphone. The players started to collect on the green, either nodding their heads to each other or shaking hands.

"Can you welcome Brenda Mackenzie with her 10-year-old son Chip on the scoreboard?" Brenda waved and Chip hid behind his mum.

The tournament began!!!

Jeremy and his husband Lionel were always the best dressed. Jeremy was the club captain and Lionel was their star player. As the tournament went on, more ale was consumed along with even more cake. The crowd cheered when Lionel's bowl kissed the jack, and the tournament was over. Their little village had won for another year.

"Can I have everyone's attention? Congratulations to our team for winning. Can I have your appreciation?"

The crowd got out of their chairs, and Jake and Sammy barked, which was their way of cheering.

"So, the winners of our best … competition are as follows:

Best dressed bowler goes to … Lionel.

Best dressed partner goes to … Jeremy.

Best behaved dog goes to … Jake. (I'm just as shocked as you, reader, but he's been an angel, and his mum's chocolate brownies may have swayed the decision.)

Best behaved child goes to … Chip Mackenzie.

Tastiest cake goes to … Coral's chocolate brownies. Thank you, Coral, I'm about a stone heavier.

Best stall goes to … Maureen Higginbottom. Thank you, Maureen, for outdoing yourself on last year.

It's now time to open the buffet and turn on the disco," Kenneth said with a little squeak.

Reader, are you ready to dance one last time with Jake … and this time … Sammy!!!

Cause the players gonna play, play, play, play, play
And the haters gonna hate, hate, hate, hate, hate
Baby, I'm gonna shake, shake, shake, shake, shake
I shake it off, I shake it off

Rachelle nudged Coral's arm. "Look at those two. If I didn't know better, I'd say they were singing and dancing."

"How many bowling blondes have you had?"

They both giggled.

Sammy looked at Jake. "Jake, you are my best friend, and I couldn't have done all this without you."

Jake turned and looked into Sammy's eyes. He paused …

"Morning, treacle."

THE END

EPILOGUE

When Brian and Sandra and the other astronauts landed back on planet *Cavia Porcellus,* they were given a hero's welcome. They had successfully harvested enough grass to last months, and they had a plan to grow grass which would save them all. The whole planet was waiting for them. The councilman gave them all a medal and said that a huge monument would be erected to them where the spaceship was built. The spaceship would be housed in a special museum to honour the expedition, and school children for generations to come would hear about their mission and its success.

Brian told the councilman how the big blue planet was actually called Earth, and it was run by very clever dogs who showed them how to grow grass from seed and how to keep sowing the seeds for future generations. With the help of their new friends, they had saved their species. The whole planet was so happy. Sandra and Brian were happy too, but a part of them missed their new friends and the time they had spent on Earth. The celebrations went on into the night. The day was declared a national holiday, and everyone would be given the day off work on that day every year.

Sandra and Brian were getting very tired, so they made their excuses and left the party. They walked home in complete silence. They were a little overwhelmed. Had it all been a dream? Had they really travelled to Earth to save their planet? Maybe they would both wake up tomorrow and realise it wasn't real.

They opened their front door and walked into the kitchen and there, sat on one of the stools, was Margot, Sandra's mum.

"Hi, you two, have you been anywhere nice?" She knew exactly where they had been. She was trying to be funny, trying to break the ice. "I've come back. Being on the road with a hoover salesman wasn't for me."

Brian and Sandra just stared at her, not knowing what to say.

Margot carried on. "Now you're famous, you're not boring anymore. We'll have so much to talk about — you can tell me all about your adventure."

Sandra turned to her dad and kissed him on the cheek. "Goodnight, Dad, I love you." Sandra climbed the stairs and went to bed. She knew her dad would do the right thing.

"Goodnight, Margot. Make sure you are not here when Sandra wakes up; you are not welcome in this house. You'd better get back to your hoover salesman. Sandra and I are better off without you." At which Brian climbed the stairs himself and went to bed. About 10 minutes later he heard the front door bang. He sighed, hoping he had done the right thing. He didn't want to upset Sandra again.

The next morning when Sandra came down for breakfast, she never mentioned her mum, so Brian never brought it up. Clearly, in her eyes, her dad had done the right thing, and the matter was settled.

She knew she had a job to do now she was home. "Dad, I need to go to the school today to see the pups. I want to teach them how to play the games Jake showed us."

Brian totally understood — he loved playing those games too.

The next few weeks passed, and Brian and Sandra missed Earth. They missed Jake and Sammy, and they realised that they had nothing on their planet but so much more on Earth.

"Dad," said Sandra one night, "I need to talk to you. I want to go back to Earth, back to Jake and Sammy. I don't want to go back to labelling at the supermarket. I think we'd have a better life."

Brian sighed. "I feel exactly the same. Let's try to go back to them," he said. "I'll talk to the others to see if they will take us back."

Sandra cheered, then realised this whole plan hinged on the others.

"Go back to bed and try to get some sleep." Brian kissed his daughter and sent her upstairs. They both potentially had a big day tomorrow, paws crossed.

The next morning, Sandra heard her dad leave the house. It was early when she walked down the stairs and saw a note on the table.

Gone to talk to the guys about going back. I won't be long. Just in case they say yes, pack essentials. I love you, Dad xx.

Sandra paced back and forth from the front room to the kitchen feeling sick and excited at the same time. After what felt like hours, if not days, Brian came back.

"They said yes! We leave in an hour. They are going to do the checks now. Have you packed? Did you think about switching off the water and electricity?" Brian said in a panic.

"It's all done, Dad, don't worry," Sandra said, calm as ever. She hugged her dad and they made their way to the supermarket car park, where Douglas, Gordon and Eric were waiting.

"Wait there. I'll be back in a flash, Gordon," said Brian, running into the supermarket.

He came back five minutes later with some carrots and lettuce. "We may need this."

They all climbed aboard and started their checks.

5 … 4 … 3 … 2 … 1 … lift off!

The spaceship landed in the park, out of sight, of course, and Brian and Sandra said their goodbyes. They all wished each other well.

"I hope Jake will want us," said Sandra, suddenly thinking this wasn't a good idea.

"Here's a beacon, Brian. If you ever change your mind, press it and we'll come and get you," said Douglas, hugging his friend.

Brian started to walk to Jake's house, picking a cardboard box up on the way. He placed the box on the doorstep and they both climbed inside, placing the carrots and lettuce to one side.

"Jake, let us in!" shouted Brian, hoping that with Jake's amazing ears, he could hear him. Jake barked.

"Who's there, Jake?" Coral said, opening the front door. "Bruce, there's a box here on the doorstep," she said, rather puzzled.

"Open it," he replied.

Coral opened the box and to her surprise …

"GUINEA PIGS!!!!"

Did this book help you in some way? If so, I'd love to hear about it. Honest reviews help readers find the right book for their needs.

About The Author

Deborah Fox lives in Yorkshire with her partner Paul. She currently works for a large electrical distributor as well as being a budding author.

Like many children, Deborah spent her time inspired by stories from A. A. Milne to J. M. Barrie, and to this day, her favourite story is still Winnie the Pooh! Her writing talents didn't materialise until later in life, as most of her childhood was spent dancing and performing.

Deborah's passions are the outdoors, gardening, interior design, dogs and cinema. She has always been intrigued with all things supernatural, and the time presented to her during COVID, coupled with the inspiration from the sad passing of her dog Jake, was the start of her first novel, *Second Hand Rose*.

With the support of family and friends, and Blossom Spring agreeing to publish her story, it has fulfilled the dream to become a published author and has given her the encouragement to write more stories.

X - @debmac730
Instagram - @defoxauthor
Threads - defoxauthor
Facebook - Deborah Fox - Author
Website - www.d-e-fox-author.com
YouTube - @DeborahFox-Author

www.blossomspringpublishing.com

Printed in Great Britain
by Amazon

47378771R00098